AF292228

Ming Shu was born in a medical doctors' family and is well educated. He works and lives in Carlisle, Cumbria. As an alternative medicine practitioner, he loves science and literature. Combining life experience and energetic thinking, he would like to be contributing more literary works to the public.

Ming Shu

CLONE LADIES

AUSTIN MACAULEY PUBLISHERS™

LONDON • CAMBRIDGE • NEW YORK • SHARJAH

Copyright © Ming Shu 2023

The right of Ming Shu to be identified as author of this work has been asserted by the author in accordance with sections 77 and 78 of the Copyright, Designs and Patents Act 1988.

All rights reserved. No part of this publication may be reproduced, stored in a retrieval system, or transmitted in any form or by any means, electronic, mechanical, photocopying, recording, or otherwise, without the prior permission of the publishers.

Any person who commits any unauthorised act in relation to this publication may be liable to criminal prosecution and civil claims for damages.

This is a work of fiction. Names, characters, businesses, places, events, locales, and incidents are either the products of the author's imagination or used in a fictitious manner. Any resemblance to actual persons, living or dead, or actual events is purely coincidental.

A CIP catalogue record for this title is available from the British Library.

ISBN 9781035829361 (Paperback)
ISBN 9781035829378 (Hardback)
ISBN 9781035829385 (ePub e-book)

www.austinmacauley.com

First Published 2023
Austin Macauley Publishers Ltd®
1 Canada Square
Canary Wharf
London
E14 5AA

There was a large horizontal banner hanging above the high gate: *"Welcome to the International Science Symposium."* Beside the gate, there were three smartly dressed ladies: one white, one black, and one Asian. They were hostesses preparing to greet the attendees of the conference.

A large square in front of the gate was virtually fully filled with cars. Attendees stepped out of their cars, carrying briefcases, smiling and greeting each other, and headed toward the conference entrance.

The hostesses welcomed them, one after one, and handed each of them a seat card.

Guests gradually reduced, and the square got quiet. Hostesses looked from this side to that side; the only thing could be seen was the fluttering of colourful flags around the square.

Suddenly, a red car speeded in from the left side of the square. The driver was a young lady. She was driving hurriedly and looking to her left side for a parking space.

Meanwhile, a black car came in from the right side; the driver was a young man. He looked to the right side to find parking, too.

Line by line, the place seemed fully occupied, and it was really difficult to find a space.

Simultaneously, they both found a space – actually the same space, and it was big enough for two more cars parking. They drove towards there from opposite. The red car got into the space first, and the lady manoeuvred to save enough space for the other driver. Just then, she heard a bang with her car.

She got out of her car as the young man hurriedly got out of his. They saw that her car's wing mirror was bent. As they both looked up, they were stunned.

"Julia! How could it be you?" the young man said excitedly with a touch of embarrassment.

"Yes! Philip! Got you now! Where you've been hidden for three years!" Julia said accusingly.

Philip shied and lowered his head, tidying up his tie and shirt. He's about 1.8 metres tall, with white skin and a clean-shaven face, bushy eyebrows, large eyes, and a towering nose.

He's about 34–35 years old. His dark hair was a mess, and there was one button lacking on his shirt.

With a dearly loved mind, Julia stepped forward to get closer to him but stopped hesitantly. "Didn't sleep well last night?" she asked instead.

Philip felt a little relaxed. He glanced at the lady standing in front of him shyly. In her early thirties, about 1.75 metres high, slim, blond, and blue eyes, a small dark mole on the left side of her chin, and a light green gown covering her bright white skin, with intelligent, pure, and elegant temperament.

"Why you late too?" Philip asked rhetorically.

"I got the conference invitation unexpectedly yesterday, so I had to prepare a speech rapidly over the night. It was finished by dawn. Oh, we need to hurry to the meeting now!" Julia said.

Philip let Julia get out of the path first, but Julia waited for him when she reached out of the lane, and then hand in hand, they arrived at the gate. Hostesses welcomed them there.

A widescreen showed the portrait of them, followed by the words "full". The hostesses followed the couple together and entered the meeting hall; the gate behind them closed automatically.

The meeting has started. The seating card became bright in the darkness, guiding Julia to find out her location.

Philip's seat was two rows behind her diagonally.

A banner above the podium said, "Discussion topic: What is the Top Priority?" in English. On the left side of the stage, at the desk, sat three men, a white, a black, and an Asian. On the right side, a large screen showed the live image of the speaker.

"The top priority is to stop carbon dioxide emissions urgently, stop all coal, gas, and fuel, and only allow green energy, like solar and wind. The problem of carbon dioxide emissions has been put forward for several decades, but so far, there has been no effect. The sea level has risen rapidly, and a large number of Earth creatures are exterminating. And the temperature of the sea is high enough to chase sharks to go ashore for food. Can we just be sitting here and waiting for the disaster to come? We can hardly rely on the lazy actions of governments, especially in Asia, Africa, and some Middle Eastern countries. They pour black smoke all day. In the name of science, we would like to urge the United Nations to impose sanctions on those," a white man with a beard said.

"It's not fair to talk like this!" An Arabian man stood up. He walked towards the stage and grabbed the microphone. "You should strongly criticise the west rich countries, as they first sacrificed the earth! After their industrialisation, they restrict other countries. That was very unfair! They set wars around the world that left poverty and hunger, but they do not allow damaged countries to set up their own factories!"

"No, sir." A black moderator came from the left side of the podium and gently asked the Arab to leave. "This is not the United Nations Security Council. We are not here to discuss political issues, okay?"

The Arab clearly refused to leave, the atmosphere of the meeting was restless, and the noise was increasing. Later, the white speaker stepped down off the podium with dismay.

"Please, let me say something!"

Suddenly, someone raised a hand from the attendee seats; it was Julia. When she stood up, the hall became quiet immediately. All eyes are watching the beautiful and elegant lady walking gracefully towards the stage. The Arab stopped sulking and walked down calmly.

This surprised Philip. Watching his beloved girl walk to the podium in warm applause. He stared excitedly and uneasily, preparing to listen attentively to Julia's speech.

Julia's portrait was showing on the big screen. She had long eyelashes, a dark-coloured mole on the left side of her chin, and big and bright eyes that spoke of beauty and wisdom. Before starting her speech, she glanced at the audience with a kind, honest, and respectful sight. Her charm drew warm applause again.

"We have no time to tangle with the past now. The doomsday clock has moved even closer to midnight. Disasters to destroy the earth are at hand. The urgent task of establishing a scientific moral examination system quickly is more important. To oppose and prohibit some kind of scientific activities that may bring harm to mankind. We must face the grim reality; let all mankind work together to save our earth!" Her opening remark drew new great applause.

"In the latest few hundred years, human civilisation had progressed rapidly; while constantly improving living conditions, we also dug out the grave of our civilisation!

"The Internet was originally used to promote the development of science and culture by sharing information, but it was greatly used by some organisations to oppose democracy, to steal technology, to suppress human rights, to make false news, and spread pseudoscience.

"The cell cloning technology was originally used to make alternative organs to help hopeless patients, yet were used by someone to engage in human-animal crossbreeding and another experimenting. We condemn such immoral scientists and such studies!"

Her serious voice echoed in the hall.

Some of the attendees bowed heads; an old man took out a handkerchief. All the audience was silent, waiting for her to continue.

Philip listened carefully; a blue vein was bulging on his temple.

"There are too many things we have to do, the most important of which is that we should push legislation in the early stages of scientific research; to prevent and stop any wrong scientific or technical acts which could be harmful to humans, even if such research seemed to have some benefits to mankind."

The audience in the hall was shocked, and suddenly, a stormy applause burst out. The Arab stood up and applauded excitedly. Philip was all adrift, sweat dripped from his forehead, but he clapped his hands too.

While Julia continued her speech, Philip's mind flew back to the past.

"Ha-ha!" With the sound of the girl's laughter, Julia, with a small braid knotted with a white bow, wearing white sneakers, and a blue-coloured dress, sat with a group of schoolmates, including Philip, who was in a black school uniform. They shared reading a book under a tree.

(Slightly older Philip and Julia) "What's your plan for after graduating college?" asked Julia, with short wavy hair, in a black velvet jacket and a sweater with the pattern of little red flowers in green leaves.

"I will continue to study biology, especially space biology," Philip replied quickly and surely. He looked very handsome, his eyes flashing. He's also in black velvet. The pattern was silver and gold.

(More mature Julia and Philip) Under the lights, Philip was more handsome, and he was reading Julia's letter affectionately.

"Dear Philip, Cambridge University is so beautiful! But perhaps it can't be compared with your Yale. Just outside the window of the library, the breeze blows, and small bridges overflow with water, green trees, safflower, and birds. Tiny dog…Come on, my boy, let's see who will be walking better in biology!"

Another stormy applause woke Philip back from the past memory, and he raised his head suddenly and found a lot of reporters around the podium, clicking flash of cameras.

In the applause, Julia's words can still be heard clearly, "Under the big banner of scientific morality, the global population scientists are united to make great achievements in proportioning of the populations and the balance of genders!

"The space scientists are united to have a great achievement for the quick and safe migration of human beings! The global biological scientists and the medical experts work together to find ways for preventing and curing the giant bacteria diseases, bad virus translations and great achievements on extending human life…"

Her clear and sweet voice was punctuated with stormy applause. After the end of her speech, the meeting had a break. The audience stood up to greet the talented and pretty young lady, together with reporters that surrounded the stage, expressing exciting feelings, congratulations, and requesting a picture with her. She kept looking up to Philip while trying to meet everyone's demands.

Philip could only stand outside of the crowd and wave his hand to her frequently. Just when he hardly got close to Julia, someone called him from behind.

"Hey, Philip!" It was a short, stout man in his 50s, balding, in casual clothes, speaking with a Slavic accent. "Would you come over here, dear?" the short man said in an unhurried way but with a bland expression and a gruff voice.

Philip retreated and turned his head to Julia, and said, "See you soon. I'll pay for your car repairs!" Julia looked at him with pity.

On a country path, not far from the main road, where farmhouses were built with herds of cattle and sheep, they ate grasses freely and, from time to time, yelled "Muumuu" and dogs looked after them like the police.

"It's safe to speak on the road nowadays," Mr Boris said to Philip as they were walking shoulder by shoulder.

"I have no time for talking today, Mr Boris. You know, my girlfriend and I haven't met for three years, and we just had a reunion today," Philip replied.

"Yes, yes. I understand it as well as I myself got a lot of things to do. Moon miners are making trouble, Indonesian Bali villa is waiting for me… Oh, afterwards, the elements of human life, as someone says, is having the best food, plenty of money, and enjoying life with a lover."

Boris took out a pile of notes from his pocket and stuffed them into Philip's hand, as well as a small delicate box, "Get your money bag bulging. All ladies like shopping, and a gift, here is a valuable necklace for your girlfriend." Then added. "Can't be stingy anyway!"

Philip took them and inserted them into his pocket, and said, "Thanks."

"I admire your lover, she's the best biomedical scientist in Britain, and you're the top bioengineering figure in the States. You are entitled to have everything! But, so far, do you know how she got to the conference? In an Economy class flight."

Philip stared at him and said, "How did you know that? Do you have a detective after me?"

"How is it possible, my genius? You are now the pride of the world, you do not cherish yourself, but we should do it carefully. We are only in the distance to protect you. But never interfere with any of your privacy," Boris explained.

"Since you knew everything, you must have heard what Julia said at the meeting. I was worried when she mentioned the clone skills. I felt something uncertain…" Philip pretend reluctantly return the money and gift back to Boris.

Boris rubbed his eyes like a little bug flew into them so he didn't see Philip's acting and just replied, "It's not that complicated, my big genius! As she mentioned about proportioning of gender and migration to space…can you find that what we are doing is not part of the task as she said? Moon miners making trouble just because they want women! 20,000 men have been there for so many years! The law does not allow sending the Earth's females there. So we must do the job of helping Lunar male workers and actually supporting human migration to space. On the other hand, you know, some countries in the world are having severe trouble with gender imbalance. If we use the clone technique to help them, is that what she mentioned?

"Someone says, 'The great desire of humans is to eat, drink, and love.' How incisive it was! Oh, so late, you should go now. By the way, we have repaired her car mirror."

Philip looked at him in astonishment and slowly drew his hand back with the note and gift box. Boris made a face and walked to the side of the road to play with the sheepdog like a child, and Philip went back very quickly.

There was popular dance music in the hall, and clusters of young men and young women were practising dances following the rhythm.

There was a lectern in the innermost part of the hall. On its right side was a large screen, and on its left was a DJ desk.

Just as so many pairs danced vigorously, a whistle blew, and a black woman about 40 years old, with dark hair, dignified and beautiful, appeared on the screen, smiling and said, "Hello! Everyone, Maria will tell you some good news: the Angel Cup Grand Prix-specific provisions have been sent to your email box. I hope you read it and take action on time.

Fill out your form according to the requirements and send it back ASAP.

"Note that the figure should be accurate, such as the total number of cells collected and the effective percentage, the classification in the screening program, the improving nourishment, and so on. The winning rate is very high that the top prize is a helicopter." Maria's notice cheered the hall.

In fact, Maria was speaking to the microphone on her office desk, and there was a lot of staff in the office working on their own desk.

Maria continued, "According to statistics, the average salary of our company last year was three times higher than white-collar workers in first-class countries. Once Dr Philip's new project starts running, our company will have an unlimited future. All right, that's all. Have a nice weekend!"

There was jubilation in the hall.

Philip sat at a desk in his office, having a video conversation with Julia on the screen in front of him.

"Weekend? That's great! I've forgotten all weekends since I left you. I'd like to spend the weekend with you last time, but you left immediately after that conference," Philip told Julia with regret.

"Oh, as I told you last time, I was unexpectedly attending the meeting and accidentally met you. So I can't change the timetable waiting for you, though I wish to stay with you."

Julia said, "I'd never known there is a beautiful Matera island in the Atlantic Ocean, nice southern European views, and a big Boris Company there. You've been hidden there for more than three years! You perhaps have a big role there, I guess," Julia said with a witty smile.

"I hope my Julia will forgive me, and I am sure you will do that. I always remember what you said when we were in junior high school, 'avoiding does not mean forgetting'. I need to avoid you for some time to achieve some goals to surprise you, Julia. At the moment, I only can say that you can cut a ribbon for our house, a marvellous, palace-style building, soon. Wish you can arrange a date as soon as possible, then I can pick you up from anywhere in the world," Philip said.

"As we are together, everywhere is beautiful. Let me see…In another month," Julia said, thinking.

"Another month, July 16, it's your birthday. We haven't been together to celebrate it for three years now. I'll fly to pick you up on that day If you agree." Philip snatched the topic.

"All right, honey! Never forgot when we were in Carlisle, celebrated our birthdays together every year," Julia said.

"Carlisle, our hometown! It's a deal now…Take good care, and let us work hard for a better tomorrow."

"You repeated these words from primary school to college, and now! All right, I'll see you then!" Julia disappeared from the screen. Philip left his seat with joy, making several stretches. A female robot came in and sent him a cup of hot coffee.

As soon as Julia's video call finished, Boris called in. "Happy weekend! I saw your work plan sent by Maria, and I feel very satisfied. Sincerely looking forward to the success of the implementation!"

"Thanks, boss, for the encouragement. I've known the pressures on you, so I enforce myself to keep working hard, hoping to break through the last bottleneck quickly. Then, the first cloned woman with thought and language ability will be a reality on the horizon soon."

"Dr Philip! Your wisdom is enough to solve even much bigger problems than this, but in the depths of your heart, entangled by so-called science morality, that hinders the smooth progress of your thinking."

"Yes, boss, you're right. I know that. It is absolutely possible to increase hundreds of thousands of clones a year if I do not have such an interference factor. But I am afraid of being scolded by the world, even more, afraid to lose my only loved woman. You know, she was born in a noble family and so elegant and beautiful. I accepted your job offer actually to get a high salary and favourable treatments to make a happy life for her. But I also often worry that once she knows the truth about my job, will she understand and support me? This is the real bottleneck."

"I understand you! The earth is round, and many people always emphasise the side they see but deny the existence of the other side. The word 'morality' is often used by someone to suppress dissenting people. On the surface, the scientific community does not advocate human cloning. But, in fact, they are all doing it!"

"Everyone is tacitly aware of it. It is clear that human cloning is firstly beneficial to human beings. For example, in some countries in the East, there is a huge gender imbalance. In one of them, about 60 million young men cannot get a wife because females are lacking! Is it horrible? Is it moral or immoral if we clone such a number of females to help them for balancing?" Boris continued.

"Let's look at the space career; if we want to migrate humans to space quickly, there must be a large number of male pioneers, as it is too dangerous for females. So sending women was banned. And many male workers living in the outer space are lonely all year round. Should they live with suffering? If you don't help solve the problem, the speed of human emigration will be delayed! Is that moral or immoral what we're doing?" Boris continued.

"Those lunar employees are complaining all the time that they want women; they say if we don't solve it, they'll go on strike. The lunar Uranium, the Lunar Helium, their one day's GDP equals one year's on the earth. That is the economic fundamental for a space career! Twenty thousand single men are living there. How sad if you just have money but no love?" Boris said, excited.

"Just yesterday, I had to promise the Lunar Uranium Union that I would send them 6,000 clone ladies in six months. Mr Philip, you know, I don't have the confidence. Actually, you are the only one who has the true authority to say so."

Philip listened, thought, and interrupted Boris. "Don't be pessimistic. I have figured it out. What we're doing is very moral! Since I can figure it out, it would be 'a hundred folds do not return'. The first batch of 6,000 cloned women, sending to launch within six months!"

"Thank you so much, Dr Philip. Whenever you speak like this, I see victory soon. Oh, by the way, as I told you last year, about 200km away from my Bali Island villa, we bought a nameless isle near the resort of Dan pasha, where one of the most modern buildings of a villa has been done. That will be a gift for you and Julia to celebrate the first batch of clone ladies sent to space."

"Thank you so much. Everything I do is for her. I want her to enjoy the happiness as a princess," Philip said happily.

"We are the same, very grateful for her. All your hard work here was for taking our super preferential offer was actually for her."

"That's true. I just want her to live in a paradise, but don't let her know what I've been doing."

"Well, Philip, you made me laugh in tears. Now that you are on the thief's boat, take out the thief's courage to achieve your goal! Indeed, many countries are doing the same research as we do. The United States, Japan, Britain, China, Russia, and Italy are all engaged in it! However, our company is the best. One day, people will respect you as much as a God! Good night, dear."

Philip's eyes shone firmly.

A large oval brown wooden table was set up in the middle of the hall with Ancient rattan chairs around the table. Large floor-to-ceiling windows lined both sides of the hall; it's double-illuminated by sunshine and chandeliers.

Maria and the other four women, Philip and the other five men sat around the table. Maria just clicked her mobile phone, and two female-like robots pushed trolleys in and sent every participant a porcelain plate loaded with tea and snacks.

Philip wore a light blue casual dress, black hair, white skin, thick eyebrow, and bright eyes, totally unlike the malaise when he crashed Julia's car. His speech was very gentle and clear, "In the last three years, our branch has provided a large number of cloned organs to the world and helped countless patients. In order to promote the early migration of mankind into outer space, we have launched special cloning, and we have built up the foundation and trained related staff.

"Employees of each apartment normally only know information which is linked with themselves, but people here around the table, we must know as more as it is better. Sometimes have to come together to discuss overall problems. A lot of people thought I had more power than a master, but in fact, like everyone, we all work for the boss. The advantage of working here is that our income is particularly generous, and once the new product has developed successfully, our income will be rising geometrically."

The participants applauded, and the atmosphere was very active. Philip ate first, and others followed, finishing tea and pastries. Each plate was equipped with wet towels and dry tissues for cleaning.

After the working lunch, Philip spoke again, "What I'm asking you to discuss today is how we can send 6,000 cloned women to the moon in six months."

After a short silence. Mr A started his speech, "Collection and selection is the first process, so to complete the task for them is not in six months but in the first month, only one month, preferably in half a month."

He continued, "During the training, we've been told to collect female somatic cells from those aged between 4 to 8, healthy girls and, in case about 35% wastes, we totally have to collect cells of at least 10,000 and visit an area which has about 100,000 population in just half a month, although the system has 500 workers, I think the task is a bit of tough..."

Philip said, "Thank you very much. It's really difficult; I think I should give you 20 days extra. How about the home cells collectors? I mean, sperm collection, is that easier than this procedure?"

"Yes, that's fine. We will distribute 10,000 kits to both the sperm team and egg team quickly," Mr A replied.

Lady A said, "The definition of memory resection, could you clarify it again? In the past, your direction was only one procedure – choice and removal, but the new document added two paragraphs 'no removal' and 'complete removal'."

Philip said, "Yes, you are right. 'Chosen removal – choice and removal' was used for training. Now the boss is in a hurry to assign the task, plus some new progress from our study so that the removal methods can be changed.

"By the way, I'd repeat some key principles about our new programs. In the world, a lot of organisations have studied clone skills for many years. The most successful was Briton, who created cloned ship Dolly. But all those manmade lives have three more common problems, unhealthy, short life, and lacking the ability to speak and memory. Our clone lady will be healthy with enough life years following design. Most of them have language and memory like a normal human."

His speech led all participles up to high spirits, and then, he carried on.

"When Briton created clone Dolly, scientists just used female eggs and nuclear and womb, no male, and original nuclear got from an old and unhealthy sheep.

"Ours is totally different. We collect somatic cells from healthy small girls and male sperm will be involved, especially we'll collect cells from specific body points when we need to do special study. Thus, we will confidently achieve our goals.

"First, if the cells are collected from healthy limbs, we don't need to remove any part, transfer them directly to the next system for nourishment, it's called 'no removal', the result is those cloned products can have a human body but no memory nor speaking.

"Second, where the cells are collected from the ear, we must remove its ideological part thoroughly, which means 'complete removal'. The aim was to clone out the same products as the first group, no memory, no speaking.

"For scientific research, sometimes we need to do 'select removal'. That's the third way, choose the cells not from limbs, just cut it's 'subconscious tissues', and keep anything else.

"There is another 'no removal' group; those cells are collected from a small girl's ear and then directly sent to the nourishment system. This result would be surprising the world because the cloned person is totally the same as the original person: have emotion, memory, and can speak. But this style of clone technology is only for scientific experiments at the moment. I need someone to help. Can I suggest Garry in charge of this job?" Philip turned to Maria as if to ask her permission; Maria nodded. All attendees applauded.

And lady B asked a question, "It is much clear. But it's too sad that clone people's lives were so short."

Maria said, "All clones are just products, not human beings. We treat them without mercy, just products."

Most attendees stayed silent, lady B looked especially sad.

"Don't be so sad, I understand your feeling. But we can change our minds in another way. When we do any job, physical or mental, we will sacrifice our energy and life, and huge body cells die for it. Now, we sacrifice a little human's cells to build up a new human future; that's worth it, don't you think?" Philip said, and everyone's eyes brightened, and they smiled.

Lady C said, "According to the document, in order to shorten the product cycle, their life can only be one-twentieth of normal people, so their gestation period will be shortened into two weeks."

Philip said, "Yes. After entering the foetal nourishment system for days, the fatal period is completed, it is considered to be a one-year-old child, and after that, every 14 days, they will grow up for another year. If they are alive for four years, they will be equal to normal people 100 years old. Any new questions, everyone?"

Maria said, "Okay, now. Other systems, please still stay here to carry on discussing. Collecting and selecting system can go back to your branch. Time for you are very important now!"

All participants applauded; someone got up and left, someone remained on the seat, and Philip continued to sit in his position.

In the centre of the hall where young people danced last time, there was an oversized round table with a huge birthday cake on it which was surrounded by colourful candles. The hall was full of flowers, balloons, and ribbons. A large eye-catching slogan was on the screen: Julia, have a nice birthday!

Julia, accompanied by Philip, walked down to the hall. Maria and a group of children came up to welcome them, and they greeted the group. A birthday song was heard in the hall, and a lot of young men and women came from different corners, holding flowers and walking around Julia and Philip.

Julia was very happy to say "thank you!" to everyone. All of a sudden, a group of robots dressed like men or women came up and brought candies, drinks, and napkins to everyone. Maria recommended Julie and Philip to go to that round table.

Maria and a lot of young ladies and young gents asked Julia to blow out the candles. After the couple did, all of the excited fellows together cut a slice of cake and tasted it.

Julia said, "This is the most delicious cake I've ever tasted." Philip nodded happily and tried to say something, but his mouth was stuffed with cake.

In laughter, Philip and Julia thanked all people in the hall and then went away from the table. The robots rushed to sweep away cups and napkins, and the large table was automatically folded. The hall immediately became a ballroom.

Philip and Julia started their dance steps, and everybody joined them, following the music; youths randomly paired up enthusiastically. Maria danced with a young man, and she watched Julie and Philip again and again.

"It's great, you're well prepared," Julia and Philip muttered to each other while dancing. Julia looked at Philip with deep love.

"It's a small celebration, but you are worth the biggest celebration. I'm sure we will be happy for our whole life," said Philip.

Philip sometimes sneaked out of her sight, at times, stealthily looked at her, and occasionally, the eyes of the two ran away from each other. After a couple of times, Philip's eyes changed with a strong sense of confidence.

"A lot of people have got married in recent years," Julie made a little complaint.

Philip answered without thinking, "I'm sure you'll wait for me. I miss you every day. I push myself to work better to achieve my life goals. We got two palaces, one on the earth and one on the moon. We'll study and work for science and love each forever."

"What are you saying?" Julie was surprised and quickly turned away from Philip. Philip was scared.

Julia walked to the big stage and said something to Maria at the D. J desk. Then the screen showed Julia's image with a microphone, her long golden-hair, beautiful mole, wearing a light green dress, slim figure, big blue eyes, long eyelashes, and even white teeth. In the accompaniment of the music, she sang a song.

> With pleasure and fondly:
> "Soul Never Separated"
> Every time you make no sound,
> I don't know how sad it was,
> The nightmares during long nights,
> Not as strong as you can imagine.
>
> Youth will eventually be old,
> The reunion should be most cherished,
> May the soul hold each other never separated?
> Like the sea ripples of water.

On the big screen, there were frames of footage from her memory, all about her and Philip:

First frame, the teenagers Philip, Julia, and two other friends. Philip drew a big circle line with white chalk on the cement ground, which surrounded an ant. Each time when the ant came near the white circle, it hesitated and turned away to look for another way to go out. Julia gently hit him with her hand and blamed him for mistreating the small animal.

In the next frame, those friends got together again. They seemed a little older than the last frame. The dishwasher drain was blocked. A girl poked it with a bamboo pole, but the more poke she made, the more clogged it became. Philip went away and found an empty plastic bottle he then circumcised its neck, made the diameter of the bottle mouth consistent with the diameter of the drain, then used the reverse pumping method, and immediately the sewer was relaxed and unobstructed.

Philip looked at Julia and listened to her singing. He was so touched and could not control himself, he went to the stage, kissed and hugged her. Maria and the audience applauded, whistling and cheering.

Julia and Philip waved their hands to everyone. They shook Maria's hands and kissed her face, and then the couple, hand in hand, walked out of the hall. The crowd waved hands with flowers saying "See you soon" to them.

A green wilderness, the distant sea flashed white. Near the middle of the lawn was flat land, and a small helicopter was parked there.

Philip and Julia, in yellow navigational clothes, one after another, entered the cabin. Philip checked the cabin, then started the plane departure off, heading to the sea.

Loose and tidy, like in a luxurious car, there were two seats in the front row of the cabin, just to suit the couple.

The cabin was so quiet that they could not hear any noise from outside. They talked as if sitting in a private capsule.

"Where are we going, Philip?" Julia asked.

"Up to you, I remember what you said once that you'd like to go to Italy. How about taking you to the island of

Marina to have a sunbath? It'll take about 20 minutes of flying," Philip replied.

"No problem, only if we are together, everywhere is a good place. Honey, how long can you keep flying? I mean fuel," Julia asked.

"Oh, theoretically unlimited mileage, graphene-powered plant, of course, we still have to check it routinely," Philip replied.

"Wow! How good it is! Zero pollution to the environment!" Julia, very happy, smiled and asked again. "How safe is the navigation? Although I could swim, I've never swam across the sea."

Philip turned his head to her with a funny smile and told her, "It's quite safe, although it's small and light, it has the same wind resistance as a large aircraft. I've never tried landing on a surface of water."

The sky was clean, and they looked at the sea below, hundreds of sails traversed through. Julia leaned on Philip's shoulder.

Philip focused on flying the plane but kissed Julie's face from time to time. Both of them were singing Julia's song, *Soul never separated*. Looking out of the cockpit, from far to near, an island appeared. The island was getting bigger and bigger, gradually; a beautiful town Marina could be seen more clearly, a winding high way around the town, sports cars on the seaside avenue, shops by the roadside, hotels, and signboards on the high slope. The beach on the outskirts of the town, boats in the sea, were becoming more and more clear, a lot of people swimming and surfing.

"I like surfing, too, Philip. Let's go surfing today, okay?"

"After you, honey, but we're not familiar with this area. It's safe to row a boat."

"You are the guy saying that you listen to me, but actually, I have to listen to you!" Julia gave Philip a gentle bite on his arm.

Suddenly, Julia shouted, "Oh, something happened to the lady down there! She fell off her skateboard into the sea and away from the crowd, people can't save her! What shall we do? Can you try landing on the sea? Or, you fly lower and slowly, and I can jump into the sea to save her?" Julia said in a hurry.

Philip did not speak, he kept getting down the helicopter and adjusting direction until he saw the girl struggling tenaciously in the sea and, at last, climbed onto a lone reef of the shoal.

They breathed a sigh of relief. Suddenly, Both Julia and Philip saw a big snake swimming towards the girl closer and closer. Philip moved his finger at this critical moment, and shot out a mass of sputum from the plane to the sea that held the girl left the reef and hung her in the sky, and at last, pulled her into the cabin.

Julia was stunned to see the scene. Following Philip's demands, she removed the soft sponge adsorption from the girl's back, helped her lie down, slanted into Julia's seat, and she herself climbed to the back row and held the young lady with her hand. After a moment, Philip parked the plane near the beach. The girl slowly recovered from the shock.

While weak, she thanked the kind couple and then borrowed Julia's phone and called her aunt in Italian. Later, she told Julia in English that her aunt sincerely thanked them and invited Julia and Philip to her house near here.

"Thanks for her offer," Julia said, "let your aunt pick you up for a rest, and we'll go home very shortly. We won't bother her."

As soon as they said a few words, her aunt drove a car and arrived near the helicopter. She stretched her head out of the window to thank and invite the couple again. At this time, the aunt was speaking in English. The two refused her invitation politely again and again, so the girl had to say, "Well, have a good time! The weather forecast says strong wind and heavy rain later afternoon, pay attention for your safety!" The girl entered the car and was taken away by her aunt.

"Such danger that girl was in! It was so scary, it made my legs weak and shaking. I'm afraid I can't swim or skate today. Please go hire a boat, bring something to eat, drink, and then enjoy the fresh sea air and sunshine. I'm going to tan my body, and listen to your stories."

"Yes, everything is up to you!" Philip went out and Julia slanted on the long sofa behind the pilot seat.

After a while, Philip brought two bags of food: lobster, crabs, watermelons, pizza and mineral water. He took it to the boat first. He touched the sampan, it felt too hot, so went back into his plane and woke up Julia who had dozed off.

While having food and drink, they talked to each other for a while, sitting on the beach near the helicopter.

Later, they took a walk around for a while and then reached the seaside, and boarded their vessel. Philip untied the boat from the berth and set off to sail along the bay.

This was an electric sailboat. Philip started the sailing key, a few minutes later, they were offshore, farther and farther away, and the figure of Philip's helicopter was getting smaller and smaller. Philip controlled the rudder. Julia lay next to

Philip, looking curiously at Philip who seemed confident and calm.

"What's that you shot to rescue the girl? I'd never heard of it." Julia looked up at Philip and asked.

"Oh, that's one of my small inventions. It's not worth mentioning as it's not perfect yet. We can temporarily call it Root Glue as my principle was to imitate a plant's root, using special material to adsorb a target without harm, trying it for rescuing or capturing purpose, which may have some use," Philip explained.

"Not worth mentioning?"

"This is really a small matter and not perfect yet, for example, it can adsorb only one target at one time and also need to see the wide big area of the target's like people's back."

"What's the big task in your heart?" asked Julia, looking Philip in the eyes.

Philip answered thoughtlessly, "The biggest tasks are to contribute to mankind's escape from the earth, and built up the best villas for my Julia, one on the earth and one on the moon. Julia is the master and I am the servant, and then enjoying the happiest life for ever."

"I am already enjoying my happiest life, nothing unhappy," Julia said.

"Not really," Philip said, "at least we are all worried about the dangers of the earth! Once you can get to our moon palace, we'll hold a wedding ceremony there!"

"That will take many years," Julia said doubtfully.

"It won't be long! Our earth palace has been done, and the moon palace is half done."

"Oh?" Julia wanted to speak but stopped.

The sun was shining, the sea was full of sailboats and the boats of the coast guard were passing through sometimes.

A seagull flew down to Julia's side and pick a ham sausage away.

Philip was at the helm, with one of his arms embracing Julia. The couple were so content in enjoying the nature's beauty and the warmth of the love.

Pinching Philip's leg, Julia said, "Oh, I still have a lot of questions to ask, almost forgot it! Can you give me a clue about what you've done in recent years? If it's not a business secret or something."

Philip answered quickly without thinking, "Promoting faster human migration out of space."

Julia was stunned, "Can you be specific, we are in the sea, no monitor near you."

"We were so far in cloning human organs, except brain, tongue and retina, we can almost clone everything. But when we started, it was under great pressure, we had to do an experiment under top-secret conditions, so I couldn't even get in touch with you. Nowadays, apart from food, the world's second needs were our cloned organs," Philip replied.

"Tell me, what role have you played?" Julia asked.

"Ha-ha, I will be always a student. In cloning organs, I solved the problem of dense structures, such as the regeneration of cloned teeth in anyone's alveolar."

"Great, my Philip, looks like you've contributed a lot to science, but I won't allow you to take part in immoral research."

Philip was stunned and immediately responded, "If you give me approval, I can clone out living, talkative person quickly."

"Is it possible? How can a clone be exactly the same as a real person?" Julia didn't believe that. "Can a cloned people have a soul, thoughts, emotions and memories?" Julia questioned again.

"I found that ordinary somatic cells can only clone bodies without souls. If we collected cells from special parts of the body that can clone human beings with completely consistent as their original person and have ideological emotion, language and memory."

"This is terrible! If Hitler is alive, will take you away and clone him as a soldier for war? And Bin Laden will find you, too. Then you're a sinner," said Julia, and she continued, "but I know you'll never want to do those research."

"Honey, I remember all your statements at the General Assembly. But on the other hand, isn't it good to clone a huge number of women to help countries where serious gender imbalance that led millions of men to not have wives, or to clone people to do tasks that can't be done by neither humans nor robots, such as deep-sea operations or outer space travels?" Philip said.

"The academic community have had a debate on this controversial research, such as moral issues, and clone's personality issues. But so far since no one can clone a replica of humans, as you said, so no one has taken it seriously," Julia said.

And she went on, "If there are such cloned people, who are doing tasks that a man can't, but they aren't treated as a man, it will be a problem, both morally and legally."

As Julia began to think about something, several seagulls slanted down and grabbed all the food by side her and another flock swooped down treating Julia as their food too.

Julia had to stand up and fight with these fowls, but as she chased them more as they come more. Philip had to leave the rudder and help Julia to disperse so many seabirds.

The boat deviated from its course and floated to the open sea. The sky suddenly darkened and then brightened. They could see a big view of the city, streets, pedestrians, and vehicles seemed clear on the right side of the boat.

Philip shouted, "No, a mirage! Our right side is the deep sea, no city there! This must be a mirage, forced by a big storm. We have to land quickly," as he said this, he turned the rudder and made the bow toward the left, Julie ran to the middle of the boat to lower the sail, and the boat turned smoothly and galloped straight to the coast.

The dark clouds like a huge bowl, covered the sea, only the waves twinkled white. Just as they were approaching a reef, a row of returning waves pushed their boat to deep sea again. Philip clenched the rudder handle to keep the ship from floating away. Julia continued standing by the masts to keep the sail low. Suddenly, a huge wave rushed over the deck and swept Julia into the sea.

"Julia!" Philip yelled, immediately loosening the rudder handle, jumping into the waves, and fiercely swam to rescue Julia.

Julia was a good swimmer; she tried to save herself in the valley of the waves. Philip came after her, just as he vaguely saw her head from the waves but a scraped big tree floating divided them. He couldn't waste time swimming around it, yet pushed the big tree away and struggled to cross over it so he could find Julia easily. Prickles stung his arms, hands, face and neck and they started bleeding.

He had to change his style of swimming to relieve the pain, the big tree was finally pushed away; he accelerated to catch up, and again and again, called Julia's name.

He was getting close to Julia, Julia heard his voice and tried to meet him, but something like a sheet of textile floated to her and entwined her, she had to struggle with the textile. The more she struggled, the more she entangled.

Philip's arrived on time, he made all his strength to tear off the textile, and the couple were able to reunite. When they touched fingers, both of them were exhausted, and they tried their best to hold hands together, smile appeared on their faces then, and sank down simultaneously as just then, the coastal rescue boat arrived in time, and saved them.

After being rescued, Julia and Philip returned to their helicopter, it was swayed slightly by strong winds.

They boarded in and changed their clothes.

"We can't go back today. The wind is extremely strong," Philip said to Julia in the cabin seat.

"That's what the girl warned," She said, "it will be strong wind and heavy rain later afternoon. The forecast was accurate!" As they spoke, Julia's mobile phone suddenly rang, and it came from the rescued girl. "I called you several times. The wind is wild and extremely strong, my aunt is worrying about you, and again, inviting you to come and stay with us tonight. The weather will be fine tomorrow."

Julia glanced at Philip and said, "Great. How can we get there?"

"Please wait just five minutes, my aunt coming is to pick you up," the girl said.

Philip went out very quickly to make the helicopter's anchor more secure. The young lady and her aunt's car arrived very quickly just after Philip completed his checking. The girl jumped out of the car to welcome Julia and Philip. The aunt opened the window and stretched her head out to do her greeting.

Then the girl sat next to her aunt and the couple sat in the rear seat of the car.

"It's better to drive manually. We all have automatic cars in the United States. In fact, all drivers still need to keep their eyes on the front and other side. Sometimes, it feels boring," said the girl.

"The size of our Marina is too small that automatic driving will take us into the sea," her aunt replied, which made everyone laugh.

Very soon, they arrived destination – Apollo Grant Hotel.

They got off the car, and felt a breath of fresh air, Julia and Philip looked around and found that this hotel was in the best position of the town and one of the tallest buildings.

Standing in front of the hotel, they could see more vehicles and pedestrians. The appearance of the hotel was very magnificent. But not busy today, there were no customers' cars parked, and no customers going out or in. Looking through the big windows, you couldn't see any guests or waiters at reception working inside as normal restaurants or hotels should.

Julia and Philip followed the girl and her aunt walked into the hall, where the furnishings were very magnificent, carved mahogany seats, and transparent crystal dining tables, and the hall was extremely spacious, but only a middle-aged man greeted them respectfully, and more respectfully to aunt.

Walking through the hall, the four people climbed to the second floor by elevator. After passing through many rooms, the aunt pushed a door and opened a beautiful room and said to Julia, "Welcome! I'm Adeline. First of all, thank you for saving my niece, Emma. This room is for you. After you settle down, please go to the dining hall, which is diagonally opposite to your room. Emma and I will be waiting there for you two."

She gave Julia the room key and pointed in the direction of the dining hall.

After tidying up, Julia and Philip walked out of their room and came to the dining hall. Adeline and Emma greeted them warmly. Adeline and Emma looked at Julia and Philip, Adeline in surprise and said, "You two are the best match I've ever seen." Julia introduced Philip and herself, and then the four people sat around the table, it was already filled with more dishes, wine, drinks and fruits.

Julia and Philip first thanked Adeline for the kind invitation and hospitality.

"Emma and I will never forget your help forever," Adeline carried on, "you two will be the best friends in our live! You know, if something happened to my Emma, I couldn't live on. She's my everything."

"It's a predestined relationship. Without Emma, how can we stay here and enjoy your company," said Julia. Philip only smiled with Julia, and agree with everything she said.

"Is your business all right?" Philip asked a question.

"My aunt actually doesn't care about the business here anymore. She'll accompany me to America next month. As I start my freshman year," Emma answered first.

Adeline nodded and agreed with Emma, adding, "Emma's mother was my only sister. Their hotel in Los Angeles is much bigger than mine, it's set by Seaside Avenue and the business was very good. Unfortunately, her parents were robbed and killed by a criminal gang. A kind gatekeeper protected Emma. I often flew over there to see my Emma, she is my only child and my life."

"You've never been married?" Julia raised her glass and asked Adeline.

"Well, did you see the one downstairs? That's the guy."

"That man is okay?" Philip said.

"The Bengali was sneaked in when my father was in poor health, and my mother had a heart attack. There were three female waitresses and two male chefs in the hotel, we needed a reliable male butler for the business. My parents wished I inherited the business and to get a good young man for helping.

"Just then the Coast Guard rescued a group of refugees from the sea, the government policy was if they had relatives or employers here, they could be picked away, and that picked guys could soon become legitimate citizens." Julia and Philip liked to hear such stories, and Emma listened attentively.

"So your family went to bring this man home?" Philip interrupted.

"Yes, it was a big mistake. At first, this man was all right, as polite as you saw tonight. My sick father taught him hand-in-hand, how to do cleaning, how to do safety checks, how to treat guests politely, how to buy quality food material, how to arrange things in the kitchen, dining hall and bedroom, and so on. When he gradually mastered all that, my father let him try to be the butler and my parents then took some travelling for health recovering."

"The bad guy guessed my parents' thoughts, made passes at me many times, I ignored, and then he boldly hid in my room and attacked me after I had a bath."

Adeline wept sadly, Emma wiped her tears, and Julia's eyes were wet too.

"Later, my parents let me marry him, and he soon became a citizen. The family lived in harmony for a while, and in the outsiders' eyes, he was the master of this house.

"Hateful, this man was a wolf! He quickly tore off his disguise, and became lazy, smoking and drinking all day long. He had affairs with all three of our female employees! Two of them were married and their husbands came to the hall shouting and destroying furniture, the unmarried girl had to go to the hospital to have an abortion, and we paid for all the expenses. Reputation stunk, the business couldn't go on, and my parents died in hatred and regret!"

Adeline burst into tears. Three people surrounded her and comforted her.

"Sorry, I'm emotional today," Adeline wiped her tears. "please go to your room to have a rest, you are tired," she added.

"No hurry, your wine is so good that we can't sleep either. Why didn't you get a divorce? Let him go?" Julia asked.

"It's a big trouble. Because if he left my house, he will be homeless, it became a burden on the government and also it was a legal problem for how to divide my parents' inheritance. He was arrested two more times by the police, and just released recently when he promised to change his behaviour. Also, my priest advised me to give him one more chance and says that he was only a half-bad man. If really divorced, he might become a completely bad person, and I would displease

God." Julia and Philip both shrugged their shoulders and looked helplessly.

On a big screen, a naked man and a woman made love in bed, the woman screams, and the man constantly keeps going. After a while, the man put her legs on his shoulder and changed his position from prone to standing. After a while, the man roared, indicating that he had ejaculated.

"Stop it, Allen, I can't take it anymore," a rough man said. The three men were watching adult porn. They sat on their own bed, very low beds, made of three layers of thick mattresses. The screen was just a hanging curtain, accepting the projection of a mobile phone. Allen was a good-looking black young man.

"Guys! Let's go for a walk!" he suggested and the other two followed him immediately. leaving their beds and taking out lunar helmets, putting on their spacesuits and moon shoes, and then walking out of the room and into the wilderness.

A big bulb hung in the sky, that was an artificial sun. it illuminated the moon land and made the frozen night a little warmer.

They came to a cave under the surface of the land, a round "roof" covered the cave. Beside the cave were countless caves linked to each other. Blue bright was automatically sent out of the cave's windows. The moon streets were different from the earth, the moon streets were not straight but like roads.

When the three young men arrived at a point, a soft door opened and gave an entry for them. They came into the entry and walked on an inter-screw street, the streets were busy, with different styles of buildings, plastic trees and flowers everywhere.

They got into a door, its inside was an enormous big dining hall. Countless people sat by tables eating food, drinking and chatting. A painting on the crossbeam says: "Uranium Dining Hull 18th".

On one of the tables, men were chatting about women. A black man said, "I've forgotten what a woman looked like."

A white man said, "What's the point of a man who makes money without a woman?"

Another white man said, "I came to the moon for money, but we've been millionaires already, what's the suffering now? We need women, not money!"

Allen and his housemate sat down at a table, a woman-like robot sent them drinks and dishes, and all these guys touched her buttock.

"Oh, don't touch me. The earth's women will be here soon," the robot said.

"It's a nuisance! She said it hundreds of times," one of Allen's roommates said.

"I signed a contract working on the moon for 180 days, but I ignored that one moon day is 28 earth days. The day before I left Earth, my girlfriend and I made love for many hours, and then I asked her to wait for me for twelve months only, I believe I would become a billionaire and go back to marry her! But sadly, she's been waiting for me on the earth for many years now. We didn't know we would wait for 14 years," the man continued.

Allen said in a hurry, "My fiancée asked me on video yesterday that could I mail my semen to her and get her pregnant."

"You are the guy that has sex by video!" a roommate said, and all of them laughed.

Almost all the people in the hall were talking about women with resentfulness. Someone passed a letter asking for signatures. The letter says, "If we are not allowed to return to the Earth or you don't send us beautiful earth women in the next three months, we will all go on strike."

"Cheer!" all the people raised their hands and agreed.

"Friends of all! Don't be in a hurry!" The avatar voice of James, the leader of the union appeared on a ubiquitous big screen.

"We are the most precious people of earth and ancestors of the moon. The moon is calm and safe with no polluted environment, no thunderstorms and hail. After generations of effort, the moon will become a human paradise. We work only two hours a day but can earn money equal to 1 year on the earth.

"Yes, we also need tenderness from women. Now I am very seriously telling you: 6,000 beautiful girls from the earth will be arriving in about 10 days. These cloned ladies will only be for our uranium miners. Boss Boris has said, they will be continuously sending such ladies to the moon. So let's be patient, keep calm and enjoin life and work."

"Hope it is true this time!" someone shouted.

"It seemed to be true, as he gave the specific date and number. It's so quick, unexpectedly!" another person said.

Marina Island, Apollo Grand Hotel. You climbed onto the third floor through an aisle, then stepped out a doorstep, it was a quite spacious roof balcony. Standing there you could overlook views of the city. The back of the building, not too far, across a big gap, is a small hill, coconut trees and cork oak trees lined on its green lawns, the gap like a valley between the hotel and the hill.

Stainless steel railings surrounded the balcony, the front railing facing the main street, and the rear railing facing the hill. Another two side railings were at least 30 meters in width. This large balcony could be used for a small playground or helicopter parking.

Philip wore a vest and shorts and completed his morning run on the balcony. After running, he did a few push-ups, then walked, and then went to the back railing to pick up his coat, which was hung there.

His phone was ringing, he took it out to have a look, it just mentioned: "collect cells". He immediately went back to his room.

Julia was still asleep. He went closer to her bed sneakily, watching her beautiful face, and listened to her even breathing. Then took out his phone gently and put it close to Julia's ear and flashed a green light once. Then he retracted his hand and gently left her. Just before he stepped out the door, Julia spoke to him.

"Waiting for me!" said Julia.

"I knew you came back and kissed me, didn't you? Please pass me the red underwear and beige bra in my bag. We'll pack all dirty objects into our bag and not bother Adeline's family."

Philip handed her all the objects she demanded and kissed her on the cheek, Julia stretched out her arms around his neck, and Philip got on the bed, kissing each other while Julia was still inside the quilt.

A man in a yellow vest was mowing grass on the lawn, and two women in yellow vests were cleaning outside windows.

Inside the doors was a big office. At a glance, there were about four to five rows of desks, each row had three more tables. Julia sat on an aisle desk in the middle row, some staff were focusing on reading computers while others typing their keyboard.

On a table behind Julia, a lady who seemed younger than Julia was talking with someone on the screen, "It's the United Nations Scientific Ethics Committee, yes, it has just been set up. Yes, her, okay, I'll transfer it to her." She transferred the phone call to Julia.

"I'm Julia, Yes, we just set up. A lot of things we need to do, but it doesn't matter for dealing with what we are dealing with right now," Julia answered the caller.

The caller continues his speech, "I heard that your committee has the power to launch an investigation and further actions on unethical scientific actions. 'Clone Progress' magazine published an article in July this year, which was ranked first in the magazine, I'd recommend you to have a look at it. Thank you." After that, the caller cut off the line and left no personal ID or contact details.

Julia turned around and said to the lady behind her, "Please ask team 4 to take the time to check that article."

Before Julia turned back, the lady replied immediately, "Team 4 had taken note of that article and expressed their opinion."

"What do they say?" asked Julia.

The lady looked at her computer and replied, "They think this article has some bold scientific insights and cloning engineering ideas that seemed to involve human cloning, but more likely a great discovery of science, so keep an eye on it rather than block it roughly."

"So that! It's not an agenda list for the moment, and please remind me about it sometime later," Julia said.

"Okay," replied the lady.

It's the same meeting room and the same table. Except for Philip, Garry and Maria, all the other attendees were new faces.

A long face young man speaking, "When we collect cells, we use Dr Philip's multi-sample method many times, it's quite speeding up the collection processing."

Philip interposed, "Good. The hidden box in the mobiles we sent you can store 100 specimens safely for 3 days. I used this way on the day before yesterday and collected 3 cells at one time without her knowing. Of course, normally, we should let the donator know this clearly."

"Dr Philip talked a lot about genetic surgery last time, and many people would like to ask you to repeat it to make us more aware of special knowledge." said a round-faced young man.

"Good suggestion! You can refer to the article I published in the journal 'Clone Progress' in July. There are three aspects of the core," Philip said.

"My first study shows that the subconscious is an empirical memory from past lives which were concentrated and stored and locked when we were born or life experiences before being cloned which was locked while being cloned. If such a locked part was opened accidentally, it will fight with consciousness, and a lot of strange mental behaviour will occur that disturb the normal life which is called schizophrenia," he continued, "so, in order to make a clone who will have part of past memory or complete memory, we need to cut relative part from DNA or not do anything.

"My second study was the functions of somatic cells. We normally believe the body cells are the basic of body construction, like a country's citizens. Do all citizens have the same thoughts and the same behaviour? No, any citizen is an individual as any cell is an individual too. Different parts of somatic cells can make a different human clone.

"If cells from limbs are healthy, we don't need to do any operation and directly transfer it to nourishing, these products will have no consciousness but have basic human activity like eating, drinking and kissing…

"If we want a clone having personalities like its original person, we need to collect cells from a special place, best is from the ear, and then do Chosen Operation, for example, if we cut off its subconscious tissues, that clone will only remember things happened after he had been cloned, and he also could gradually create its own memory and intelligence.

"Of course, if we collected cells from ears, don't do any cuts and directly send it to nourishing, that clone will get subconsciousness and copy all memory and wisdom, nearly 100% like its original person but only lacking in a period of knowledge of being collected from its master's body and, since after being cloned successfully start its own new life."

"Wow! How great! But if a clone we produced is the same as its master, how to distinguish them?" Garry asked.

"The distinguish essential is the master or original person have complete memory but the cloned one will have broken memory."

"Dr Philip, could you please tell us, why are we collecting cells from such young girls?" a young lady asked.

"Good question," Philip replied, "in short, it can help the success rate of cells clone. Normally through human life, cells can be divided about 25 times, in which, young cells divide easily and old are more difficult. 4–8-year-old girl's cells are the most ideal. So pick out the female cell nucleus away and replace the male sperm nucleus instead," Philip answered clearly.

"Does that control the clone's age?" a young lady asked.

"No, without male sperm, the cloned person will be ill and have a short life. We set up the clone's age mainly from control their cell dividing times through a nourishment system which made the clone's cell to not divide ever. Actually, considering both the boss and our economy," Philip answered and he continue, "I still have time to accept the last question."

"Let me ask Dr Philip the last question. Since the somatic cell is different to cells in the ear, why not collect cells from the same point?" a new young lady asked.

Philip gave her an answer immediately, "For simplifying processing and accelerating speed, the best way is collecting limb cells, but in practice, the collection team worked in a chance of convenience so we can't direct them to follow which way. But they must make sure of its category. If the cells weren't from limbs, they must be labelled and stored separately."

He took out his mobile phone from his pocket, and clicked it; a tiny metal jumped out. He handed it to Garry.

"There are three specimens. Please check them first, if the qualities are okay, then give them 3 different treatments. 1. Completely cut out the ideological part, 2. Selective, cut out subconscious tissues 3, Don't do anything, directly sent to nourishment. And register their electromagnetic tracking number."

"Okay. Thank you for giving us so much information, it will be a great help for our job. Dr Philip," Garry said sincerely.

Bengali knelt on the ground and pulled Adeline's skirt. "I know I made too many mistakes, no it's a crime, but God won't let me die, and still left me alive with my beautiful wife. So I want to change myself, please give me one more chance, a last chance. I want to make achievements. During your stay in the United States, allow me to continue running the business. I will be running it as well as father-in-law had done."

Adeline hesitated for a while, glanced at the guy, and then dropped a bunch of keys on the ground for him.

"For God's sake, I'm giving you the last chance. Try to find chefs and waiters yourself. Keep cleaning, record accounts carefully every day. I'll come back and check you without notice to see whether you've really changed." With that words, she walked out of the hall with Emma.

In a crowded bus, two middle-aged women in colourful blouses were talking in the front row.

"Why the bus is so crowded today?" woman A asked.

"You don't care about the outside at all! A large number of refugees came again, and this time the number is the highest in history. The authorities are mobilising business owners and householders to accept refugees for work as quickly as possible. Wages can be slightly lower, and employers do not have to pay employer tax. That's why traffic is busy," woman B said.

"All right, just these three people for me today." In the camp, two men and a woman were recruited by Bengali. The camp master asked him to sign it, and then he led them to come after him to Adeline's house.

Standing in the hall, he said to the three recruiters in English, "Listen, I used to be a refugee too. I won't bully you. Now we need to resume business, start with less staff, do a good job firstly and then will have more staff."

He appointed a man. "Now you're in charge of the kitchen." And turned to the other man. "You're in charge of the cleaning job at the moment. I know you're a good chef too, when our business resumes, I'll let you do your chef job."

Then, he looked at the note on his hand and said to the woman with a smile, "Oh, your name is Alisa, I love beautiful women the most. Your task is to dress up and be in charge of the reception in the lobby. Don't be afraid, no one would dare to bully you, because I am your security guard."

Finally, he added, "Guys, please work hard. If any customer comes in, serve him well and try to make a temporary passenger to a regular customer. I'd say it again that the first month's wage depends on the business as my boss didn't leave me a penny."

The neon lights of the hotel were bright again. Apollo Grand Hotel was reborn. Drivers and pedestrians were attracted. With the big size neon lights, through glass doors and windows, people could see a new beautiful woman inside the hall, which made people more impulsive to enter the restaurant and the hotel.

"Oh, oh," Alisa welcomed customers with her pretty smile. Natives can't understand what she saying but just like to chat with her.

Sometimes Bengali came to join talks or help to explain something, he said to a gentleman, "Sir. You must be a charitable person, and if we don't help the refugees, we displease God. At least, at this point, I'm sure you'll stay and we'll definitely offer you the top-rate service."

The first customer was successfully retained, and then, more and more followed.

Maria wore a bamboo-blue blouse, she had a full chest, a round face, and white teeth, she held a red phone answering a caller, "Boris Cloning Company, yes, last year, we sent more than 100,000 cloned hearts, it is suitable for any size body, the weight is only 10 grams. Hmm? Broken limb accessories? Please send us the 3D images and we can make a clone of it and ship it to you within five working days."

The red phone was just put down. A blue phone rang up with green flashing light.

"Oh, you are an Asian agency? What? To clone women? Who said it? Need one hundred thousand? I'll tell you later after I got my boss's answer."

As soon as the caller was gone, the black phone rang, "Oh, Mr Boris! I just mentioned you, huh? That's true! A great deal! Yes, it's going here. Dr Philip really figured it out, and he's been doing well to win the two palaces! He loves his sweetheart very much!" she continued. "The speed of collection and selection is so quick that it'll be entering the nourishment system tonight. Okay, thank you, boss. Bye!"

The green sea and the white sand could be viewed from afar or near.

The palm trees, deciduous trees, and egg flowers appeared everywhere and the men and women in the distance are sunbathing, swimming, boating or surfing.

In an old grass-top cool shed, there was a large square table. Boris sat beside the table with another billionaire, Mr Davis. Both of them were naked in their upper body, with a big-sized towel wrapped around their lower body. Each of them has two young Indonesian women accompanying them and two men-servants standing a few steps away. On the table, full of fruit, dishes, wine bottles, and soft drinks. Sometimes servants, men or women came and asked about adding something, and ladies will help them pour wine and get dishes and clean their faces and mouth.

"Boris has a sharp eye! I'm impressed. When the network sales destroyed our financial group, you built up a clone industry and started a new era of human history! You're now one year's GDP equal to a middle country's figure!" Tall, white, round face, and a wide chin, Mr Davis wore dark sunglasses and raised his wine glass.

"Thank you so much! Never forgot your great help, Mr Davis! Without your support, I couldn't turn over. When I started the cloning business, you gave me $5 billion in one sum," Boris said and continued, "Dear, Davis, you are a real giant in business, you understand humans, you were never worried if I bankrupt when you gave me the great help." Very sincerely, Boris raised a glass to Davis.

"Luckily eye-catching hero," Davis laughed and said.

"Almost all capitalist has original sin, and should also take risks to atone, grow, or fail. Real capitalists are actually harder and risk much more than migrant workers! People only see the scenery and enjoyment of capitalists for a little while, but never understand the unparalleled contribution they do to society! We are both qualified capitalists!" Davis raised his glass again.

"Mr Davis has a good opinion of me. I have a good opinion of Philip. You two saved my life," Boris said.

"I really want to know how did you get him! Such an honest and intelligent young man."

Boris pointed southeast and say, "Right over there, 100 miles from Dan pasha island, we bought an unnamed isle and built up a most modern palace for Philip and his girlfriend. We also gift him a helicopter. He's worth it! Only when you met reliable talents you can make capital growth rapidly."

Davis looked at the direction, and praised Boris, "Great, so generous, Boris! I heard you have also built a palace for them on the moon."

"Yes, it's completing soon. Unfortunately, there is no dust on the moon, so it cannot be refracted like on the earth, otherwise, the appearance of its pictures must astonish earth people!

"We'll only need to do more decoration inside. Philip will go to the moon with his girlfriend for marriage. If we don't understand his inherent needs for wealth and reputation, we can't get him."

"How long does it take Philip to fly from Matera Island to Dan Pasha villa?" asked Davis.

"His helicopter is graphene powered, with almost permanent flying, plus some of his own inventions made it more advanced. And its speed is 3000 km per hour. He can fly from Matera's garden dorm to Dan pasha villa in about 20–30 minutes."

"Do you think he's going to clone a woman like a real person and succeed?" asked Davis.

"I absolutely believe it, absolute success! I think Philip may be the world's most talented scientist. I'll give you a small example: My dear wife had cut off her breasts because of cancer, you know, that's a terrible consequence! Mr Philip cloned her absolutely natural, beautiful and even better breasts than the original! He helped countless people regain their happiness life!"

Suddenly, there was a strong gust from far to near, followed by heavy rain and thunder lightning, the thatched pavilion began to shake, and the waiters and ladies hurriedly helped the two old men leave.

Collection and selection department. They were all young staff. All of them wore light blue overalls, blue hats, light blue masks and light blue gloves. Everyone had an oversize desk with a screen and micro-operation facilities on it. The robot trolleys shuttle was around visiting all the desks, sending them new specimens and carrying away semi-product trays.

The specimens were placed in a tiny glass tube that was placed in a transparent tray. Each tube has a symbol outside, a red symbol "from ear" and a green symbol "from limbs".

The staff took over the tray and examine the green symbol under the microscope. If it was normal, the green light flashed, and the staff put it on the left side of the desk and let the robot carry it to the nourishment system. Occasionally, the specimens were unhealthy, a red light flashed, and staff put that glass tube into a drawer under the desk on the right side of him.

For the specimen of the red symbol, the staff clipped them out with tweezers and did the operation under the microscope. The screen showed all processing vividly. After the operation, some kind of liquid was sprayed onto the wounded specimen and it was reloaded in a glass tube, then the tube was placed in a box, the box in front of the staff.

Each time the robot sent new specimens to every desk and took away boxes from the staff's left, front or drawer on his right, then put them in different cabins. These cabins have labels: L means from limbs, E means from ears, D means done operation, and R means rubbish.

A black girl, a little chubby, was focusing on her work, she seemed very skilful, and a robot praised her by saying, "You're the best!"

Just when the robot left, her screen flashed, and a girl of the same age, the same skin cried to her on the screen, "Geris, don't be scared. My brother got into a car accident just minutes before. He broke both legs. He can't dance with you at all."

"What?" Geris burst into tears. "Say it again, did that just happen today? He danced with me last night." Geris was dizzy and confused, without any checking, put all specimens in the L box, and just let the robots take them away.

She was suddenly alerted, aware of her mistake and immediately called a special number, she told the listener that she had made a mistake, her face flushed and crying.

The soft lights shone on the magnificent room, not by any bulbs but from every inch of the building material. Philip dressed in soft clothes, sat in an automatic rocking chair. He was answering Maria's report in his moon home.

Maria's portrait on the screen was very clear just like in the earth. While listening to Maria, Philip looked at the earth-moon time indicator. After Maria finished speaking, Philip replied calmly, "Don't let the news spread, and we can only solve it when clones arrived on the moon, I guess the same thing happened in the first group of clones as well. We can only pray to God that it doesn't happen again!"

Just about to change channels, Maria returned to his screen and was very happy to speak again, "When are you coming back to see the first clone kids? They are two years old now and are waiting to set off!"

"Okay, I'll come back to earth now! Please report it to Mr Boris and inform related systems," Philip said.

"Okay, I'll do these right now." Maria disappeared from the screen.

Philip calculated something on his mobile phone, then stood up, looked at the time indicator, and tapped his phone, quickly three men came in.

"Hello, Dr Philip!" Three men welcomed Philip, and one of them introduced another one. "He's Mr James, the chairman of the lunar uranium union."

Philip shook hands with them and said, "It's nice to meet you in my moon home."

"Have you got rest? I mean, sleep." James asked.

"No, I daren't sleep here. One day on the moon is equal to one month on the earth, a lot of things waiting for me to do on the earth. The moon time is so slow and too long, so I understand how lonely and boring for a single man living here is," Philip said.

"That's true. Employees are angry and complain all the time. Just an hour before, Boris told me that cloned women will arrive soon; the miners should be satisfied with it. Boris and all workers here appreciate your great technology," the chairman said.

"I should thank you all! Something needs to be declared that cloned girls are collected body cells from ordinary girls, which removed their ideology from DNA, so clone girls are just better dolls with some life actions. They can live on earth for four years, but about 50 days on the moon. However, we will continue to send new ones to you. I just heard an accident happened that a few specimens didn't get through checking, the results, perhaps a few cloned ladies will be like normal women who got memory and sense. If anyone got such a clone, don't be surprised, treat her like a doll, not a real person."

"Why do they have so short life?" one of the three men asked.

"The aim is to make your workers feel fresh all the time. That's what the boss is most concerned about," Philip said, the eyes of the three men suddenly brightened.

"As the limited capacity of the spacecraft, we can only be sending the ladies when they are in small size, so after arriving on the moon, they need to take another few days to be mature enough like 14 years old. I hope you'll understand," Philip added.

"Don't worry about this. Boss Boris told us. It is our pleasure to send the first group to our miners," James said.

"Uranium is the heart of the company. The company relies on uranium to support the outer space career!" Philip said with a smile. And added, "It's time I go back to earth now. As soon as 6,000 ladies are delivered, then the second, and the third, it will be endless. I like living on the moon, quiet, no wind, no sand, no dump, no bacteria or virus, it's impossible to get sick!"

James and the others shook hands with Philip and left. Philip pressed his phone and called for the lunar taxi, "Please take me to the Earth Station."

Julia was answering a video call at her desk "Oh, yes, the United Nations does not yet prohibit human cloning, but we are starting a concern about whether there are any ethical issues in such studies. Cloning human organs to help patients is a good thing, but we need to prevent anyone from using that technique in the wrong way. And all we can do now is to use scientific ethics to check and measure the activities of those practitioners or organisations."

As she put the phone down, it rang again, the caller told Julia, "The sea level has soared, and many islands, including South Asia, the South Pacific Ocean and some islands in southern Europe have been seriously flooded."

She was dazed for a second, then replied, "When the heavy rain stops, we will depart immediately for visiting and prepare to help some damaged areas."

From a distance there was a group of people, Philip, Boris stood side by side with Maria, Garry, and someone else. They were watching robot nannies push prams one after another, each trolley has a baby lying in it. Through the transparent safety cover, all baby's faces were flushed and looked very healthy. Boris and everyone seemed very happy.

Garry took out his phone and clicked twice, then three robots came over and pushed special prams with identification tags on the covers. Garry walked with them to Philip, "Dr Philip, these are your three special girls."

The three girls' faces were obviously as same as their original. Julia, each one had a mole on her left chin.

Philip asked Garry to hide their identify tags, and then asked Boris, "Boss, could you please guess which of them was completely cloned with no operation?"

Boris said embarrassed, "It's hard to guess it now as they just are two years of age. It'll be easier to guess if it's three years old. Only Dr you can tell us!" Everyone looked at Philip.

"It should be this one." He pointed to one of them, just she frowned her eyebrows and waved her hands for few times. "Only her. Her act shows that she has a mental activity that comes from the memory of her past life. The completely removed one has no activity at all, and that resected one needs longer time to establish her own consciousness and memory, not for now."

Garry uncovered their ID tags, it showed that Philip was absolutely correct. Philip held Garry's hand and said, "Sent that no conscious one with those 6,000 together, and please continue to take care of another two, I'll rearrange them soon."

"Okay, do the tracking continue?"

"Yes, they are all important objects for our study."

Philip turned to Boris and said, "I've arranged moon nourishment works for clone ladies to ensure they are mature enough and nourish a couple of days when they arrived there."

"Let's go, for a walk," Boris suggested, so Philip followed him, waved "goodbye" to the others, and they went away.

On the beach, Boris and Philip sat on a clean rock. Boris took out a bunch of glittering keys from his briefcase and handed it to Philip, "These keys for Dan pasha villa. It belongs to you now. I think when you get a chance, be there for a fantastic holiday and have a good rest."

Philip humbly accepted the key, "On behalf of Julia and me, thanks boss, I will continue to do my best!"

"What's the life plan for those cloned ladies and what's your next plan?" asked Boris.

"Here are two computational principles. First, in the course of a normal person's life, somatic cells can be divided 25 times, so normal people could live multiple about 125 years or so, but we had skills in the nourishing process that make those clones only be ultimate cells means they can't be divided anymore so their life is only about 4 years age in the earth or 50 days in the Moon. The normal foetus period is about 275 days, but for current clones only 11 days, after the foetus period, they will get one year old every 14 days. Short life for a clone is somehow sad, but they'll have some good conditions such as no wind, no rain, don't need hard work, no bacteria or virus…they'll spend most essential life on the adolescence years."

"Oh, I see! Thank you, Dr Philip! In fact, you've helped the company design a blueprint! You give the short life for clones indeed to promote the company's production. You didn't mention it, but I understand it. We have to strive to develop productivity!" Boris said.

"In terms of research, what I thought more often was: how can we do re-clone? Re-cloning is breaking the natural limit so that the ultimate cell cannot continue to divide. If we can get success in it, then we don't need to collect human cells again. We just collect cells from cloned ladies on the moon, and then we can make countless clones and send them to other planets."

"I also thought about clone-back research, that was even more crazy. That is using the ultimate cell to replicate the original real person. If this dream becomes true, the human life will be quite prolonged."

Boris was very excited about what Philip said.

"It's so inspiring that I'm worried about how long I can live. While I'm alive and healthy, to pick cells from my ear, use your 'none operation' way and directly send it to nourishment, then another Boris will come out who will as same as me. But, oh, not now, the cloned Boris will take all my properties and lovers. No, not now. But anyway, human life seemed to becoming very interesting and very long soon! Plus we can clone any old organs to maintain people's bodies, what a beautiful future for our humans!" Boris was so excited.

"In theory, it could be done. I'll try," said Philip.

"Thank God to let me tell you! You're a genius! Let's imagine that our clients will be in the universe!" Boris said.

"Mr Boris, I'm honoured to meet you, too! You gave me the confidence to prepare everything for my dear Julia. You know how deeply I love her! Also, as a big boss, you have done a lot of hardworking, for example, sending so many clones to space was not easy to deal with and the related authorities!"

"First of all, we must understand the law and use it. The products we sending are not contraband. No one can say that they are explicitly prohibited earth women. Besides, the weight is only 18 tons and not overloaded. Therefore, applications for space release have always been approved. The space station is commercial, as long as you don't break the law, you are welcome to transfer goods every day," Boris said.

After crossing the bustling urban area, the road was separated by a roundabout toward Philip's dormitory. It was surrounded by safflower and green trees.

When the car arrived, the metal door opened automatically. When the car entered the yard, the door shut automatically. The car turned to the left and entered the garage. His helicopter was parked there as well.

Walking out of the garage, he went into the dormitory hall and then to the bathroom. Later, when he came out of the bathroom, a robot asked him, "Can I take the dirty clothes for washing? Have you checked their pockets?" It reminded him to go back to the bathroom to pick up a bunch of keys Boris gave him before.

Then he entered a wide and comfortable bedroom, a robot sent him coffee and snacks and put them on a sofa table.

He sat on the sofa, took a sip of coffee, played the key, and repeated the tune of the song Julia had sung at her birthday party. Later, he stood up to see big pictures on the wall, it's a story about fighting with sea waves, him and Julia. His thoughts came back to that morning, after exercising on the roof balcony, he collected Julia's cells from her ears, Julia said, "You kissed me…" His face flushed and he moved his head, he felt very sorry.

The Mobile suddenly rang. It was a video call from Julia. Julia stood in the rain with an umbrella. "Honey, did you know where I am now? The town of Adeline's, Marina Island. It's raining heavily here, and the sea level rose half a metre overnight, and nearly overflows the seawall. The earth is really in danger!" Philip felt sad to hear the news, Marina town was important in his life, where Julia gave her first night to him. And Emma, Adeline…he loved all of them.

"I see, my dear, I miss you all the time. I wish could fly over and pick you up immediately to my Matera garden! The Earth is in danger. Best wishes to people in the flooding area. Please take care, when you have a holiday, I will take you to our earth villa. It is on a mysterious island in the blue sea, the villa's master is my Julia."

"Huh! Why didn't you tell me earlier?" Julia said with coquetries, unstoppable joy crawling up to her cheek.

"Well, after we visited another disaster area, I'll let you pick me up to your garden dorm, but to visit the villa in later months," Julia continued.

"Okay," Philip said. The video call finished, and he over-excitedly, jumped off the sofa and lied across the bed.

A bright moon urban, not high buildings but semi-lunar buildings, beautiful and sparkling. Outside the house, manmade Sun hung in mid-air leading the moon land more bright and warmer.

Allen and his two roommates were packing their own luggage. Man A said, "I believe girls are really coming now! I'm going to make my own room look beautiful!"

Man B grinned and said, "No, not so quick. We still need to wait for them for a couple of days."

"Oh, I'll make a baby on the moon who has my colour," Allen said in a strong African accent.

"Hey, you think too much, they're all cloned women, not fertile, they're just dolls," man B said.

Man A seemed to have packed up and said to man B and Allen, "I'm going to say 'goodbye' to you now, I'll go to my new room, that belongs to me and my girl, I'm going to groom there, spend every sweet day, take care, everyone!" And then he left. Allen and man B were still carrying on with their own packing.

Matera Island, Philip's garden dormitory.

In bed, a man and a woman held each other tight and made out. Philip's coat and Julia's skirt were laid on a swivel chair, behind the chair was the king-size bed they were laying on.

After a while, Julia turned to the side and let Philip untie her bra buckle. When Philip was about to do it, Julia turned around and asked Philip, "When can we get married?"

"Oh, dear." Philip lay down on his back, showing his broad chest.

"Whenever you say. An ideal wedding in our moon palace, but I need to get the UN approval for your travelling, so perhaps it can be here instead, wedding in our earth palace, Dan Pasha villa."

"Then let's wait for a little while and I'll go to Dan pasha to have a look. We are quite busy at the moment, the organisation has just been established, and loads of things waiting to be solved. I would like to stay here with you for a few days but I have to go tomorrow. Recently many islands sunk into the sea. Don't know how long the earth will last," Julia said and turned back to Philip to unbuckle again.

"Earth's people should be leaving this planet as soon as possible. We are one of the luckiest people, as we have already got our own building on the moon." Philip said, unbuckling her bra and kissing her madly, and the room darkened.

In the distance, the city building's lights reflected into the roaring sea, mixed together and sparkling in the dark night.

The beach where Philip used a parking helicopter was flooded deeply. The sea level had been climbed up to the lower ring road. But the main roads and streets were still normal. The neon lights of the Apollo Hotel still hung high at the fork, but no vehicles, no pedestrians. It's night, the town was asleep.

Under a pink light, on a widen, soft bed, Bengali wriggled on a woman with her pretty legs separately exposed outside the sheets. She closed her eyes, and drops of tears ran down from her beautiful face to her cheek.

Bengali slid down from her body, carried his shorts, got up sweaty, and then sat next to the bed, grumbling, "How could a woman don't have that? It's so disappointing. When I choose you to come and work here, I hoped to have a good time with you!"

"I'm so sorry. I don't know what's happened to my body. I'm nearly 30 years old. I have never slept with a man. I always wonder why I've no menstruation but other women have." Alisa got dressed, sat behind him and put her hands on his shoulder.

After a silent moment, Bengali returned to calm from the loss, he kissed her a few times, and solemnly said, "Never mind, Alisa, we're still so good, at least lovers, and your body is most beautiful." He kissed her again and touched her chest and said, "It's just, you don't know, men get crazy when they are going to make an ejaculation. Someone may shot in an anus, but I never do that."

"I'm sorry, so sorry." The woman snuggled up in his arms. "Would you still treat me well?"

Bengali wearing thin pyjamas stood up, took a few steps along the bed, and answered her positively, "Of course, your beautiful and excellent service made the business prosper. Your beauty and enthusiasm are praised by all the customers."

"The world is so unfair. God knows that if your body was like a normal woman, I'd leave Adeline and spend the rest of my life with you!" He looked up at the ceiling. "It's a pity that such a beautiful woman has no vagina." He sighed.

"In the future, if you meet a woman who has a vagina, I won't be angry if you shoot in her, okay?"

Alisa went behind him and put her arms around his waist. He turned cold and suddenly hugged the woman back to the bed and stripped her clothes. The lights dimmed and suddenly, Alisa screamed, "Ah!"

Trackless trains entered the indoors, towing coaches, all the coaches were transparent, and all passengers were small girls of about two-year-old, who looked healthy but lacked something in their eyes.

A metal gate opened automatically to let the trains enter. Then closed automatically after all the coaches entered.

With a fire shining in the sky and the fog surging, rows of rockets were sent into space.

Not too far, on a pleasure boat on the seashore. Boris, Philip, Maria, and Garry were sitting and watching the space rockets. After babies were sent off, they raised glasses of wine for celebration. Maria said, "Three days later, they'll arrive on the moon, and six months later, they'll become lunar brides! That's another 6,000 cloned ladies; our boss's promise to the moon was fulfilled in doubled number."

Boris said happily, "Thanks for Dr Philip, thanks everyone, with your excellent contribution, our business is thriving! May we produce 6,000 every day to meet the human market's needs!"

"Dr Philip, one of your girls was sent out with the last group, the other two are okay, where do you want to send them?" asked Garry, sitting next to Philip.

"Please look after them for a while, I'll pick them up soon."

Philip then smiled bitterly and said, "I've given myself a problem, 1 didn't tell my loved one that I collected her cells for research that she always opposed."

"Is that hypocrisy or helplessness? The helplessness for science!" he said as he drank wine with a complicated expression on his face.

"Come on, let's comfort Dr Philip!" Boris led to a toast, and Philip soon returned to normalcy.

Apollo Grand Hotel was lit brightly, on its ground, and in the restaurant hall, all tables were fully occupied by customers, and the upstairs guest rooms were fully booked.

From outside to inside, the hotel was very clean, and every staff face was full of smiles. Three male chefs were busy in the kitchen and three lady waitresses were busy in the restaurant hall. Customers spoke different languages and raised glasses to each other in cheers. A tall white man stood up and advised everyone, "Cheers for our good luck, thank goodness we escaped the flooding this year!" All customers agreed. Alisa greeted guests when they were coming in or going out of the lobby.

Bengali, dressed in a white shirt, wearing a silk vest and a cigar in his mouth, walked to guests' tables while sending his greeting.

While busy and lively in the hall, came in two new guests, a young lady and a middle-aged woman, dressed generously with an elegant attitude. Alisa hurriedly welcomed them.

The two ladies smiled happily and went to say something, but Bengali saw them from a distance, and immediately rushed over, the cigar in his mouth almost fell to the ground.

"Oh, my boss lady! Why didn't you give me a notice so that we would welcome you?"

Seeing Adeline he smiled, and kissed her boldly, Adeline didn't dodge it, but said affectionately, "Well done, my parents' wishes succeed and I feel satisfied as well." And then he kissed Emma on the forehead. Emma looked at the scenario with great pleasure and exchanged a satisfied glance with her aunt.

"Alisa, this is our boss lady, the owner of the business and property, my wife, Adeline," Bengali said to Alisa. Alisa bowed respectfully to Adeline, Adeline looked at her with satisfaction.

"Boss lady, would you take a seat and have some drinks? Or I can accompany you upstairs. I knew there was a big locked room, I guess that's yours." Alisa's language was not very fluent but can be understood.

"Let's go to the room by ourselves. You keep working for customers. Please send us dinner in half an hour, lobster, codfish, ham, pizza, ketchup, Genoa beer, and some Chinese green tea."

"Very well, madame, I'll remember all your orders."

Adeline and Emma walked through the lobby and then went upstairs.

The pink light spread a warm glow in the room. Adeline lay on the bed in dark lace pyjamas. Bengali was half-naked with a white towel wrapped around his abdomen. He was gently massaging Adeline.

"Well, it's been a long time since I felt this good. Massage feels good, Alisa is a good worker, and all chefs and waitresses are good as well. You've rebuilt the hotel in the same way my father had done. Thank God, well, it means that people can change. I'll give you a reward. Come on."

Bengali was very happy, his eyebrows fluttered and said, "Here I am!" He took off the blanket and switched off the lights, then Adeline start groaning.

The sun shone through the windows, making the room bright, the clock on the wall was showing it was nine o'clock, but Adeline and Bengali were still asleep. The phone on the dresser suddenly rang and woke up them, it was the chef. "Boss, the price of beef has suddenly gone up, do you want to buy it or not?"

Bengali looked at Adeline, Adeline said nothing, so he immediately replied, "Buy it. You guys work as usual, I'll come over soon. Prepare us a small dining room and an English breakfast for three people."

Both of them were well dressed. Adeline smiled. "Well done. Big change. A bad slave became a big boss now!"

Bengali giggled with joy. "Thank you, my dear wife! Your merciful heart saved me, you forgave me hundreds of times!"

"Keep doing the effort! I can only stay here for a few days then I have to return to America. From my observation, you've really changed. We can tell my parents to comfort them in heaven. Tomorrow morning, after cleaning up, organise the whole family to go to my parents' grave for a memorial service! I mean not only our three people but all staff in the business."

"As you say!"

"Don't be so sweet, I know you are a naughty guy. As soon as I leave, you'll flirt with someone else. Alisa is so beautiful, can you hold yourself back? No, it's imposable, but I can forgive that," Adeline continued, "just wish you keep improving your behaviour, don't go too far. For my dead sister and my beloved niece Emma, I must be concentrating on running the Los Angeles hotel for several years, so will still let you manage the Apollo Hotel here. You must be happy for the opportunity. I like Alisa, you must treat her very well, and only her. If you hurt her, I won't spare you!"

Bengali was nervous but secretly felt happy, he listened respectfully and replied, "God will know that, although I have a lot of bad records, but my heart only belongs to you!"

Adeline pretends to slap him but said, "Get ready! After finishing business, order all staff together to set good entertaining, I have sent an invitation to my most respected friend Julia and her boyfriend to come over and have a big dinner."

"I promise! We'll implement all your command correctly! Thanks, my dear boss-wife, and on behalf of all the staff as well!" Bengali gave Adeline a big bow.

Downstairs business was very busy, on the top of the hotel, Adeline, Emma, and Bengali stood on the roof balcony, waiting for Julia and Philip to come. After a while, Emma was the first one to see a helicopter flying toward them and said, "Look, they're coming!"

Philip parked the helicopter on the wide balcony, Julia got off the plane first. Emma rushed to hug her, and told her quietly, "Bengali has changed for the better." Julia shook hands with Adeline and Bengali, and Philip did the same.

All family and staff entered the dining hall, and a large rectangular table was already set up. Adeline sat opposite Julia, Bengali opposite Philip, Emma opposite Alisa, chef and waitresses took their seats spontaneously.

First, Bengali stood up and raised his glass. "To thank the parents of our business and our family, to thank our boss-lady, my dear wife, to thank our distinguished friends, Julia and Philip, to thank all my staff friends! Cheers!"

Everyone responded to him and raised their glasses; the atmosphere was full of joy. After dinner, Alisa played a beautiful Arabic song, won praises and applause and then all friends joined hands around the table to play a group dance.

Emma was sandwiched between Julia and Philip, whispering endlessly.

The next morning, all the staff and family drove to the cemetery where the ashes of Adeline's parents were buried. Their tombstone could be seen from far away, white in colour and relatively taller than others. Adeline and Emma first got out of their car, then led others together with flowers in their hands and solemnly went to the old couple's graves.

Just as they got closer and closer to the graveyard, Adeline almost cried out in horror when she saw her 'father' alive there, it's totally impossible!

She saw three men at the grave, bending their bodies like looking for something, and one of them is her dead 'father'. "My father! It's impossible, it's impossible!" She was surprised, and Bengali saw it as well. One of the three men, the tallest, was Adeline's 'father'.

"It's absolutely true! But absolutely impossible! Huh? My father-in-law was dead and cremated. I'm the eyewitness. How could he come out again?" Bengali felt strange.

While Adeline and Bengali were hesitating, those three men suddenly recognised that they were surrounded by so many people, they were scared and ran away. The two shorter men dragged that tall man 'Adeline father', but Adeline and Bengali stopped them. "Please explain, why you are here. Why does he look like my father? What happened?" Adeline asked peacefully to the two shorter men.

Philip drove the helicopter with Julia and traced Adeline's team, when they arrived and parked near the cemetery, they saw what happened there.

The two shorter men looked at each other helplessly, and one of them replied, "Hello, madam, please don't be afraid. We are from Sheep Clone Company, and it will take a long time to explain your question in detail. Please allow me to give an answer shortly!"

"Our scientists and technicians not only clone sheep but also try to clone man.

"We collected the cells from the dead person who lied in the funeral parlour and then cloned them, we have been able to clone the appearance, but can't give clones ideology, so the clone can't speak, has no memory and doesn't know who you are. Please don't treat him as your father. He's not a man, just a clone like a doll. I'm sorry, we're leaving now."

They began to move, but stopped again as Julia called them, "Wait a moment, Please!" Julia said. "Could you tell me what is the value of studying and cloning dead people?"

The shortest man immediately replied, "To be honest, I'm not in charge of this research. I am only in charge of commercial business. According to the engineer's advice, we often bring this clone here to try to get his soul from his graveyard," he continued, "the company's researchers say that once we can clone people with ideology, they can speak, have memories, that would be of a great significance and may affect the world's laws, cultures, politics, industries, justice, medicines, arts and so on. For example, some people miss the dead very much, they would pay a big price to buy a clone if we can supply it. It will be a good deal and it will create a new industry," saying that, the three drove away.

Adeline led her group to continue the memorial service. When it was finished, Julia and Philip said 'goodbye' to her, saying, "We would like to stay with you longer, we like your small city and like nice people here, but we are too busy at the moment so we have to leave you for now. Thanks for your kind invitation and we wish you all the best!" Julia hugged

Adeline and Emma and shook hands with the others. Emma hugged her again tightly for a while, both of them in tears, at last, they kissed again and said goodbye.

As the helicopter took off, people from Adeline's team drifted away, seeing this, Julia asked Philip, "Is clone technology good or bad?"

"Hey, honey, you're tired. Take a good rest first. Please shut your eyes, I'll tell you later." Julia gently pinched Philip's arm and shut her eyes. Philip looked around, ensuring to keep her safe and avoiding the cold wind.

Boris walked on the lawn with a beautiful white dog, he threw some balls far away, and let his dog run to catch them back, later a drone flew to him and landed stably, the door automatically opened, a small robot goes out of the craft and gave him a cup of hot coffee, a sandwich and some dry tissues, the robot continues Boris' job of playing with the dog while Boris himself sat on a roadside chair for a break. Later, he took out his mobile and spoke to Philip, "Oh, Dr Philip, how about the next group of clones?"

"The collection and election are all ready, we have 10,000 specimens."

"Great, take more time with your girlfriend!"

"Thank you, boss!"

Philip sat on a desk, facing a computer, thinking about things. Just ending Boris' call, the phone rang again, it was from Garry.

"Hello, Dr Philip, the two girls, I don't know what to call them, they are 6 years old now, and they have been taught separately by different teachers. What should we do next?"

"Oh, in a few days I'll come to pick them up, you still look after them for a while, thank you for reminding me," Philip replied and then continued with his thinking.

In a pink light, on the king-size bed, Alisa's naked body, perfectly cute and delicate. She lay in Bengali arms wrapped in towels. The telephone suddenly rang up on the table, Alisa crawled to reach the table to get the phone for Bengali.

"Oh, Dr Philip! Are you still busy this late? Yes, she left several days ago, and she will not come back for three years. Emma is in an adolescent period, she has to protect her until she graduates and took over that business. Oh? Two girls? Oh, okay, I'll see you then."

He put down the phone and kissed Alisa, "You'll have something good to do soon. You'll learn how to train your children to do their homework then. Ha-ha."

"Really? What? I like children."

"Me, too. We'll be parents soon!" The two wriggled in bed and the lights dimmed.

Philip's helicopter came and parked on the roof balcony. He got off the aircraft with two identical girls, they were welcomed by Bengali and Alisa. Philip shook hands with them, Bengali said to Alisa, "You can bring your kids to the lobby to play. These kids are cultured and wouldn't make noise."

"We don't speak or laugh loudly in public, our teacher told us," the two girls agreed. Philip and Bengali watched the children jumping and being taken away by Alisa with great joy, the two men walked slowly and had a talk.

"Could you find out if there is anything special about the two kids?" Philip asked Bengali, they sat in a small room, a perfect place to talk confidentially.

"The first impression is that they are too much like Julia. They are simply like Julia. The face, the smiling, the skin, the mole," Bengali replied.

"What did you feel the other day when you saw the cloned Adeline's father?" Philip asked.

Bengali replied, "That was amazing! At first, I was surprised, and then I felt sorry. If it could speak, it would be treated as a real person, how good it would be! Well, if it's so, does he get human rights? They can be voted to be an MP?"

"There are some arguments in the scientific community, but not as much as you thought! You are very clever, such questions like clone's civil position and human rights would be argued for many years.

"But to clone out a person who can speak and think has been realised, such as our two kids you've seen," Philip said calmly.

"What?" Bengali was stunned and nearly jump out, but was hinted at by Philip. They shut the door and locked it to keep their talking.

On the big bed under the pink light, Alisa lay in Bengali's arms again. Bengali kept kissing her neck and shoulders, and she touched Bengali's bearded chin with her hand in turn.

"Do you like these kids?" Bengali asked.

"Yes! I like them very much!" Alisa replied.

"Honey, bless you! Dr Philip will fly here again, tomorrow, not for the children, but for you! To collect your cells and clone a perfect uterus and vagina for you. Two weeks later, he will take you to a place and install that on you, then you will become a normal woman, and our lives will be complete!"

"Really? Honey, I can't believe it. Thank God, thank God!" With that, both of them sat up and made a cross on their chests sincerely.

"I don't want the lovely kids taken away after their vacation, they are angels! I like them so much," Alisa said.

"Your dream come true, honey! I'll visit the best school tomorrow, to see that fat headmaster, once their new semester starts, our kids will be their students. They are our kids! I'm the father, you're the mother, and we have to take good care of them! Their names will be decided by you and me."

"It's not a dream, is it?" She turned over and bends Bengali down and she sat on him, the lights dimmed and the bed wriggled slightly.

Philip lay inclined in his bed and clicked his phone. The clone Julia in the Lunar Nutrition Centre could be seen for a minute. It now seemed like a true Julia, but with eyes blinking less and lacking content, almost like fish eyes.

Then he did another click, two clones of childish Julia could be watched immediately. They lived with Alisa and Bengali now. Their appearance, activities, and characters were totally like the real Julia when she was the same age. The "twin sisters" were sleeping.

On a big bed in a beautiful room which was decorated like a fairy world. The two small girls, head by head, were covered in beautiful sheets. They were talking, one said, "I feel strange. How and when did I get a twin sister?"

The other one was surprised. "What? Sma? You've been reading too many stories, that made you sink into the fantasy world! How can this be fake? Sleep, psychopath!"

Philip turns off the video. Then, called Maria, "You didn't go to bed? Is the new collection and selection done?"

Maria replied, "Yes, it's in nourishing now, three weeks later, they will be sent to the moon. No worries, I'm assured we can arrange such things now."

"Thank you and the other staff," said Philip.

There were dozens of participants sitting in the conference room; Julia was speaking on the podium. She looked solemn.

"The Ethic Committee has been in place for two months. There are a lot of things to do, we need supporters all over the world. A lot of problems had been accumulated in the past. Our team have only dozens of staff, so it is difficult to sort out the massive old problem, but we still can deal with current practical and urgent problems quickly.

"Once again, some people have raised doubts about cloning research. The scientists who clone animals or clone organs are now trying to clone human beings. Not sure whether cloning humans is good or bad for the earth's households, and no one has suggested stopping it. In this regard, I suggest sending someone to do some investigation first."

Julia's proposal was supported by applause and finally, they decided to send Beta, Anna and a man as a small team to go to the island of Marina to investigate the sheep cloning company first.

In a primary school classroom, which has four desks in three rows. One desk for one child. Sma was placed on the left end of the second row. She was wearing a pale-yellow bottom with a red plaid shirt and her "twin sister" Lis was sitting on the right end of the second row, she was wearing a yellowish green plaid shirt. For the twins, such an arrangement makes it easier to identify.

"Before beginning today's English lesson, let's briefly review what we learned in the last lesson. Who can come to the blackboard and write out the six words taught in the last lesson?" the teacher asked. The classroom was silent, students looked at the board, but none of them give a response.

"Lagan, can you?" the female teacher asked a tall, black boy in the last row. Lagan stood up and indicated he got a sore throat. The teacher shook her head and said, "Does that sore throat affect your writing?" The classroom burst out laughing.

The teacher turned and asked a small Muslim girl in the front row, "Asia, you should remember well, right? Come and try." Asia was stunned for a moment, then went to the blackboard, pick up an electronic pen, and wrote: day, (dad) mum, moon.

"I forgot others," she said in ashamed.

The teacher encouraged her. "Very well, but why wrote 'dad' with a parenthesis punctuation?"

Asia replied in trembling, "My dad is dead and his ash was in a box, so I used parenthesis."

"Oh, I'm sorry, Asia did good work, all right. Let's encourage her and thank her." All children gave out applause.

"Now, is anyone else coming and writing?" Sma raised her hand and the teacher nodded, she went to the podium. All the students curiously watched her walk and glanced at her twin Lis as well. Sma wrote out a lot of words quickly. All classmates were stunned, and some children shout out, "We haven't learned it yet!"

The teacher gladly watched her write and praised her. "All right, all right. Did you learn it all in the past?" All kids applauded followed by the teacher, only Lis's face flushed and she did not applaud.

In the fairy-style dining room, Sma and Lis sat opposite each other, with a lot of food, fruit, and drinks on the table. Alisa, dressed in a dark blue and white shirt with stars, gladly looked at this, and at that, and asked affectionately, "My babies, are you happy at that school, it's been a week. This is the best school in the city."

Lis says, "I'm not happy, Mom! Today, Sma scored so well in class that she overtook all her classmates. Have you sent her somewhere to learn more?"

Alisa smiled sweetly. "Impossible, please trust your mother's honesty. Lis, everyone's ability is different, don't be disappointed, maybe you'll overtake her later." The two small sisters looked at each other happily and start eating. Alisa was so happy that she couldn't express herself.

Philip and Garry sat together to watch the two children. "Doctor Philip, you're so great. What a marvellous creation it is, to collect three cells at one time, gave them different arrangements, and get different consequences! You can make a clone just to be a doll, the one on the moon is. You can make a clone remember its childhood days like Lis. What is more, you made a special clone who has all the memories, language abilities, wisdom and subconscious as same as its original person like Sma. I admire you, Dr Philip, you are my hero!"

Philip smiled calmly. "Let's learn together! However, Sma is a special clone that does not remove any DNA and seems totally similar to Julia's original. But it still has a long period of lost memory, since the cell was collected from Julia until the clone became a memorable childhood. Just like a film, the original one and the copy one, the copy one had some pieces missing, so it is lacking a lot of stories compared to the original."

Under the pink light, Bengali and Alisa hugged each other. Bengali was very happy and said, "Honey, you're exactly the same as the normal women now, everything, exactly the same."

"Yes, I really feel it. Dr Philip is so great, I know now how it feels to be a woman! I also respect Adeline, but don't know what can we do when she comes back several years later," Alisa said.

"I respect her and love her, too. It was my fault in the past. What moved me most was that she likes you; she knew we had been together, and she actually recognised it. Legally, I can get married to four wives, but I only belong to you and Adeline." And they made out.

In the teacher's office, several teachers talk about things that they find strange. A female English teacher and a male literature teacher sat on the opposite side. The male teacher said, "You know, in my literature lesson, the topic I gave was "Happy Home". Later, I find in Sma's composition, she wrote that her grandfather was a retired British police officer, and her grandma used to be a yoga instructor. I can say, none of what she wrote was realistic, but her composition was vivid, for that, I went to their hotel for a meal and asked her mother, Ms Alisa, and her father, Bengali, and both of them denied that story, but they also said, Sma was not a lying child, she was very smart and imaginative."

The English teacher said, "This child's imagination is too rich than every contemporary."

The male teacher also said, "I used to see a strange view that two different colour flowers blooms in the same tree. Sma and Lis are twins with the same outlook, but their IQs are so different."

Three investigators sent by Julia spoke to Sheep Clone delegates. Anna asked, "Did you mean that the current world-class level of cloning is your company? And the cloned human was just like that, with no speech, can't do anything, no consciousness, and no memory just like a doll? This kind of scientific research has been carried out for decades, how much time and economy has been wasted!"

"Ladies and sir, the experiment has been carried out for a long time. But we always worked in grey zones, some members of the scientific community oppose these studies, but the markets welcome these studies, such confusion really affected our career."

"Let's end today's investigation for now. You didn't bring danger or harm to the public, and you didn't break moral ethics. Perhaps we will pay attention to you in the future. Thanks for your cooperation," Beta said. Three investigators stood up and shook hands with Clone company's delegators.

"It's a weekend. We have some spare time, should we go to the seaside to have a look? Julia was there when the seawall almost broke," the male investigator suggested.

"All right, let's go and have a look," the two ladies agreed.

They drove to the beach, there were a lot of swimmers, surfers, and sunbathers.

As soon as they got out of the car, they were stunned by the sight, Alisa with Sma and Lis got out of her car, and the children carried lifebuoys. The mother and kids together went to the beach. Very beautiful mother and daughters especially the two twin girls; their outlook and spirit were a total copy of Julia, and both of them had a small mole on their left chin too.

"Hi! Can we take a photo?" Anna greeted the Mother and daughters, and then they stopped there, smiling at the camera. Beta clicked her camera, then the three investigators thanked the mother and daughters.

"What a wonder, the family is so beautiful as a fairytale! The girls are just like Julia!" Anna said.

"I've never seen such a beautiful lady, except Julia!" Beta said.

"Send it to Julia and surprise her!" after looking at the photo, the man investigator suggested Beta.

At a desk, under the light, Julia looked at the two girls in the picture with great interest. "It's so similar! I have a special relationship with this town! I'm sure I'll go to the town again," she said to Anna and Beta, they sat opposite her in her dorm.

Sma and Lis sat opposite each other at the dining table, Alisa run in to feed them, Lis was shedding tears, and Alisa wiped hers, "Don't be sad, Lis, Mum escaped from a disaster but never cried, alive or dead just in seconds, I did not cry. It's not a bad thing for you as Sma will jump to a senior level. You're not a low-IQ student in your class. It's just that Sma is a bit too high."

"Mom, what did you say? You 'escaped'? But I do remember that our family was in Carlisle, England. I haven't heard of anyone in our family who escaped?"

"Hey, my baby, of course only adults knew what happened in the past, so you just study and play with ease!" Both girls wanted to say something but stopped.

In bed, two sisters were lying together. "What else do you know?" Lis asked Sma.

"Strange, I'm 10 years old and will be in senior school soon. Why don't I believe in my memories? This is not the hometown like in my memory. Did I have any strange illness or an accident?"

"No, we are the same age, we've never been separated. We have never left Mom and Dad, and never left the hotel and the town," Lis replied. Suddenly, Lis said in a terrible voice, "Will aliens take you away one night? I'm so scared!"

"Oh, stop it, I'm scared, too!" The two sisters huddled together.

Philip was watching a video record of lunar uranium. So far, all the first group of cloned ladies were becoming "brides". These beautiful girls were carried away by men, and their body weight was "as light as a piece of paper!" said a moon man as he walked and kissed the clone girl holding in his arms.

All videos showed the same thing in the Uranium rooms: "girls" were stripped naked, pressed down and kissed feverishly by men.

Philip clicked to see Julia's clone, she was being held down by a rough man. This guy kissed her all over, then went over her and took off her clothes. Philip could not tolerate it and switched it off.

In one room, something unfortunate happened. A young man just took off his clothes hurriedly and start kissing a pretty "girl" lying on the bed, both of them felt something strange and become hesitant, suddenly, the girl sat up and said, "Martin! My cousin!"

"Yes! Rachel! My cousin!" They held each other and burst into tears.

Martin was embarrassed and put on his clothes quickly, Rachel watched him. "Martin, how can we meet here? It's like a dream, I know it's the moon but," Rachel said.

"Yes, dear cousin, but how did you come here? The UN banned sending earth ladies to the moon," Martin asked.

"By accident, we are here! You seemed just like years before, a very handsome young man."

Martin looked at Rachel more carefully, and said, "If not because of your father's disagreement, our baby would have been at least 3 years old now."

"He believed that marrying someone in close relatives would cause their kids to be born with illness," Rachel defended her father's idea.

"Dear cousin, how about now on the moon, would you want any other man, or just me? I am the best choice, we know each other," Martin said flushed.

"I don't know...." Rachel seemed a little shy.

Martin stepped toward her, and they hugged, Martin kissed her, lifted her up and then placed her on the bed.

Sweaty, Philip got out of bed, placed a towel on his shoulder then left the bedroom, and Julia quickly got up as well and put on a bathrobe and left the room too.

Philip's bathroom was painted in green hue, quite spacious, he was having a shower facing a wall mirror. Julia's bathroom was also quite large, with a pink hue. Julia lay inclined in the bathtub, wearing a bathing cap, her tender shoulders and legs were showing clearly but other parts of her body were vaguely seen in the bubbles.

After a bath, Philip sat on his couch, in a pale green silk nightgown, Julia sat next to him in a pink nightgown, a robot sent them trays of snacks, drinks and tissues. After they had eaten and drunk, Philip asked Julia, "Should we take a walk outside?"

"Good idea," she agreed.

The two walked into the magnificent aisles. there were famous paintings on the wall along the way. No bulbs, but all the aisles as the same natural bright as outside of the building.

There were rooms on both sides of the aisles. "It's a two-story building with the same number of large aisles upstairs and downstairs, some rooms have the same function such as dining rooms, toilets and bedrooms, but some rooms have different functions such as a reading room, experiment room, music room, etc." Philip gave a brief introduction to Julia.

"There are enough rooms and toilets, just for two of us, wish we have two or three children in the future," Julia said.

"Of course. everything is designed to be convenient such as a bathroom next to the gym, yet also bathrooms next to fit room and bedroom," Philip said.

Julia looked with interest at rooms, such as bathrooms, bedrooms, dining rooms, reading rooms, fitness rooms, and yoga rooms. The floor was smooth, bright as a mirror.

"Robot waiters respond to calls and answer master's questions any time, and accept master's order whenever," Philip told to her.

They came to the downstairs aisles, and some function rooms were arranged like upstairs. Through the windows, they could see outdoor gardens, sports fields, aircraft and car parking sites. They went away from the building and stepped to the gate. Beside the car parking, Julia found a special room "Robots rest room".

"What does that mean? A robot needs to have a rest?" She felt funny.

"That's the on-duty robot doing testing, charging, updating and repairing the off-duty robots."

They went through a path surrounded by green trees and colourful flowers like fences of households. Outside these fences were a seashore road, white beaches and a blue sea just in the front. Oak chairs, double or multi-seat intervals between the road and beach road and seashore.

"It's hard to imagine the price your company paid for you," Julia said.

"Thank God, thanks to boss, especially thank you. You helped me with endless wisdom and ability, so to receive such awards. My Julia and I are the only couples who had both earth and moon palatial residences, or so-called villas."

They sat down in a double chair by the side of the road. Julia lies coquettishly in Philip's arms. Philip kissed her and stroked her and hummed Julia's song "Soul never separate". A male-like robot came over and asked Julia, "Would you have tea, coffee or something else?"

"A cup of milk and little biscuits."

"Okay." The robot left.

A female-like robot came to Philip. "Give me a cup of green tea and a few biscuits," Philip said.

"Yes." The robot left.

After a few minutes, all the things they ordered were delivered.

"This villa has a huge value," Julia said.

"Entrepreneurs won't spend money on the wrong things. Last year, we sold more than 200,000 cloned hearts to human organ markets, which was one of our businesses. The revenue was imaginable," Philip said.

"I never ask about your secrets. Can you tell me a little bit about what research progress has been made recently?"

"Nothing worth mentioning. I like to study everything. One of my crazy dream is to do a re-clone and clone back. You know that Adeline's clone father was a waste, but if using his cells to clone back her original father. If there is any hope, it will be a tantamount re-alive of dead people. Then human life will no longer be limited, and everything in the world will be completely changed."

Then he continued, "There's only a thing that won't change. Julia is my only lover. Every success, me and my company, is because of you."

"What you said was so sweet! You can bring the dead back to life, and also you can sweeten the alive person to die! Go! Let's go swimming!" Julia took off her pyjamas, and change into a bikini, rich breasts, a narrow waist, long legs, golden hair spread to her shoulders, long eyelashes, big blue eyes, and a brown mole on her left chin.

Philip sat admiring his lover and lazily said, "You're so beautiful."

Julia turned to touch his forehead with her fist, scared him to stand up, and do the preparation as she did, took off his pyjamas, show his dark blue swimsuit, and walk up to her.

A team of robots came, two of them pushed rickshaws, Julia and Philip sat on each of them, and the robots pushed them to reach the sea edge.

Julia swam and Philip stood on the skateboard surfing. Drones hovered over them for protection, and swimming robots prevented Julia from deviation into the deep sea.

The sunset in the west flushed Julia's skin. "Wow! So happy! Honey! I'll be here every weekend!" She pulled Philip off the skateboard and hugged him tightly, and then they went behind a pile of rocks.

"Too busy," Alisa said to Bengali as he stood next to her, "Honey, I feel almost overwhelmed. Our business is too good!" Bengali nodded and shook his head helplessly. "Thanks to you, it's really hard for you."

"This hotel is really extraordinary! I have been a regular customer for decades. Their food is beautiful, wine is beautiful, the lobby is beautiful, the service is beautiful, ladies are the most beautiful. Have you ever seen the two princesses, their daughters, oh, my God, They're fairies!" A middle-aged female customer in the restaurant hall said to her friend around the table.

"The strange thing is, these two girls grew up too quickly, they become much taller in several days. In order to see them, I come here almost every couple of days," said a middle-aged man with a beard.

Just when Sma and Lis passed through the lobby, the guests held their breath and watched them.

The other table was full of female guests, with red wine in their hands, among them was a middle-aged woman with several gold rings on her fingers she said, "All people say fairies are beautiful, but no one has seen a fairy. Only Alisa's daughters are really angels! I'd say, with their pretty girls, this hotel will be full of guests even if they set it up on the moon."

"Ha-ha, go to the moon? There is no air, no water, how to open a hotel there?" A fat lady grinned.

"Believe in human wisdom! It is said that someone has set up a lot of enterprises on the moon, and the GDP of lunar Uranium, one day is equal to earth's one year," said a woman of middle age.

"Did you hear? Dear Alisa! God gave us all this. Love and protect our baby daughters," said Bengali gently.

"I know, but I felt it's strange too, why are my children growing so quickly?" Alisa said.

Bengali wanted to explain something, but instead, said, "Don't waste your brain. We don't think what we don't know."

A middle-aged man in a light blue doctor's overalls was having a conversation with a bald policeman. Two ladies next to the police were Beta and Anna, who had investigated sheep cloning companies last time.

"All this is true, on Sma's initiative, she found me. Let me keep it a secret from her parents, to check whether there was anything wrong with her health. She has a lot of doubts about herself. How can a child be growing more than 30 centimetres high in a few months, how can a student learn so much knowledge that the teacher had not taught? How could a child remember a lot of life experiences that are totally different to reality and her parents denied them as well? She wondered if aliens abducted her. Because she can't find any other answer," the middle-aged doctor said.

"So, what about her twin sister?" asked Beta.

"The body development is the same, but the IQ is quite different, actually Lis has a normal IQ, but Sma's is too abnormal! Think about it, in just a couple of months, the progress of study has skyrocketed from primary school to college! Oddly enough, she believes her name was Julia, in Carlisle, England."

"Can we meet them, Officer?" Anna asked the policeman.

"Yes, I'd accompany you together!"

Philip and Garry were watching the two clones of Julia, Suddenly, they saw someone tracing Sma. Philip felt like a crisis was coming. Immediately, he called Bengali. "Something happened recently. Your daughter may be in danger. Please lock Sma at home immediately, don't tell anyone, don't let anyone see her, I'll pick her up tonight, and so as Lis."

"Yes, Dr Philip," Bengali said.

Bengali quickly took Sma, who was at home, to a secret room in a corner upstairs, and locked her inside so she couldn't be found easily. When he went downstairs, Lis was gone, so he immediately asked Alisa to look for her. "When you find her, just take her home without explaining anything."

"Okay," replied Alisa.

There were five people sitting in a big car, a police officer, Beta and Anna, a male teacher and a female teacher. They first went to high school to find Sma but she was not there, then they plan to drive randomly and go back to see her later.

On the way, they happened to see Alisa and Lis walking in front of them, they parked their car on the side of the street and took a walk following Alisa and Lis.

Alisa heard something and turned her head back, she saw police and others were tracing her and her daughter. She was frightened, pulled Lis and ran away quickly.

The male teacher said, "That's Lis and her mother, that's the girl in front." They thought about the safety of the mother and daughter, and wish to stop them from running. The police called them, "Don't run, be careful!" But they even ran faster. Unfortunately, a big van emerged from the corner. Both of them were knocked down and left bleeding on the ground.

Philip and Garry sighed when they saw this on the screen. Garry said to him, "It seems Alisa wasn't crushed to death."

Philip replied. "Lucky, otherwise Bengali wouldn't be living. You keep watch. If Alisa is really alive, you don't need to let me know. I'll fly over tonight to pick up Sma with me.

She's been growing up and inconvenient to stay there anymore."

"Okay, Dr Philip," Garry replied. "Oh, wait a moment, Alisa woke up and was helped by an ambulance, and Lis has died."

Both Philip and Garry sadly made a cross in front of their chest.

When the helicopter landed on the roof balcony, Philip walked down with a solemn expression, hugged Bengali, with white flowers in his hand, and paid a greeting to Alisa, she had a bandage on her shoulder and elbow.

"We thought those people wanted to catch us, so we tried to escape. They went to the hospital to see us and explained that they didn't want to harm us and were just investigating some scientific questions. Poor Lis." Alisa couldn't help crying.

"It's not your fault, Alisa. You are excellent. You've done all the best for your kids. That was Lis' fate. Is she still in the freezer?" Philip asked.

"Transport and police said it was an accident and there was no responsible party. The authorities will cremate her when we signed. So we're waiting for you," Bengali said.

"Sign it. Please. You were always Lis's father and mother. And for Sma, I want to bring her with me, would you agree?"

Alisa seemed very sad, Bengali smiled bitterly with understanding and said, "At least we can't stop you from doing that even our hearts feel sad, you know. If you can send her back quickly. Alisa and I will be very glad, as we will miss her all the time."

Philip said, "I understand. We'll be back quickly."

Alisa opened that secret room. Sma was as tall as a real Julia now! She recognised Philip immediately and jumped at him.

"Philip! You come to see me!" Philip looked at her affectionately, and Sma looked at Philip with a youthful smile, Alisa and Bengali were stunned by the scene.

The two waved hands to Alisa and Bengali and went to the helicopter. Alisa suddenly cried aloud, which surprised Sma, and Sma ran back to Alisa. "Mum, I don't want to go!" She clung to Alisa, and both of them burst out in tears.

After a while, Alisa was calm and said to Sma, "You should go with Dr Philip, I'm sure you will be okay and will come back soon." But Sma still didn't want to go, "Mother, Father, I want to stay here with you, I'll don't want Mother to feel sad."

Philip stood far away waiting, Bengali lifted Sma up in his arm, and with tears said to her, "My Sma, we all love you, but you must go with Dr Philip now, and you'll be back soon, let Father send you there." With Alisa's help, He lifted up Sma and went to Philip, and helped her into the aircraft. Alisa raised one hand to her with tears.

Philip drove the aircraft rising and turned around above the balcony and head out of the window and said to Bengali and Alisa, "Take care of yourself, Alisa, Bengali, we'll be back soon."

Boris wore a pair of black sunglasses, with a cigar in his mouth, and sat in a rocking chair in front of Bali Island Villa, with two waitresses swinging his chair. When he saw Philip appear, he told the waitresses to stop and let them leave.

"Hi, dear Dr Philip! You'll not laugh at my bourgeois lifestyle, will you? When you are old, you should enjoy as much as you can."

Boris continued, "Let's get down to business. You may already know, the lunar mine told me of cloned girls have a little problem, one of the clone women obtained by a man, who was her brother on earth. So the brother and sister were surprised when they meet, and they remember all things in the past and were so embarrassed."

"I knew, there are a few cases because staff in the worst mood made a negligence. It will not happen again, normally but we can't promise forever as accidents may happen. I have asked James to let the brother and sister live separately and not to tell the sister that she was a clone."

"Okay, I believe in your great abilities. No one can tell you what to do. I just tell you what's going on. How's it going? Is Julia satisfied with Den Pasha villa?"

"We are so satisfied, boss. Thank you very much. The design is so thoughtful and so advanced. The most interesting thing is, Boss's villa is just near our villa which made us feel more safe."

"Enjoy it, dear Dr, you see, I almost never bother you, because you're busy enough, the earth, the moon, and, Julia."

"Oh, thank you, my good boss. Well, enjoy your life! Maria told me that the fourth batch of the cloned ladies has been sent to the moon under your command. Congratulations!"

"Thank you, Dr Philip. You are the real commander of our company!"

Julia and Philip sat in a large reading room under the fluorescent light. There were a lot of smart equipment surrounding them.

They sat at different tables and work on their own articles on the computer. Julia was writing an article entitled "Similarities between Endangered Earth and Critical Human Illness". Philip was writing an article entitled "How to deal with organisms on the moon which cannot be corrupted".

Robot-waiter delivered tea and drinks to the couple, both of them were immersed in their own work and forgot the time until the antique bell struck 12:00 middle night.

Both of them looked up at the clock, turned and smiled at each other. They stretched out and stood up. Two robots draped capes on them and said, "It's late autumn, although it is a tropical area, the sea breeze is strong, must prevent catching cold." The couple hugged each other and walked side by side, followed by robots out towards their bedroom.

"Masters, you've reached your bedroom. Your health rule is no midnight snacks, is it? All robots wish you a good night." Then the robots left them, the couple opened the door themselves.

"How I wish to be together every day. When we study together, it's quite efficient so we can improve more quickly! It was amazing," Julia said.

"Yes, my princess. At the moment, we have to work hard in our respective fields, and we have important tasks. The earth crisis would happen instantly. Sometimes I wonder, if the sea level suddenly rises madly, some area like Holland, or even small isles like Marina, would sink into the sea. If I come from the moon to pick you up, should I go to Dan Pasha villa first, or Matera dorm or Marina, Adeline's town?"

"I hate you! You know what I'd like to listen to! I really like you to encourage me to stick to my work…hmm if the abnormal sea level rises, if it really happened as you say, you should fly to Adeline's town first, rescue Emma, Adeline and other friends!"

Julia kissed Philip and began to undress, and the lights dimmed.

Sma and Philip are sitting on a lawn, Sma asked Philip "Why do I feel you look old recently? I can't believe you have a beard."

"Oh, is it?" Philip answered and thought to himself: "Funny, who growing very fast indeed." But he had to follow her and said, "Yes, I'm glad you don't care what I looked like."

"Yes, I hope you're always handsome. Isn't it better to be both talented and handsome?"

Philip confirmed that Sma's thinking and memory were exactly the same as the original Julia, then he tentatively moved close to her, but Sma pushed him away. "Pay attention to gentleman's demeanour and you can, until we were registered as a formal legal couple."

"Ha, Sma! You two are exactly the same!" Philip blurted out.

"What, what did you say? Two? What does that mean? Say it again?" Sma grabbed Philip by the ear.

Philip sat on a rocking chair at his Matera dorm. With a large screen on a large desk, he used voice control to check the Moon Uranium clone.

It was lunar daytime; the strong sun made the ground look like its painted white. The street was busy, a lot of people take walking randomly. A lot of strange traffic was driven by robots or self-driving vehicles on roads. The difference was, most pedestrians are couples now.

Philip gave a word, and Julia's Moon clone appeared on the screen. She sat in a room, with no company, the mole still on her face, but her hair was totally white, more wrinkles on her forehead, she stood up slowly, and seemed to take a walk, her back is a little bowed. Philip switch out the view and turned to watch the street.

Suddenly, something appeared on a corner of a street, and later, more and more the same thing could be seen everywhere. Philip frowned and called James.

"Yes, I just prepared to call you about this problem. It just happened yesterday. All are the first batch of clone ladies, I think they are at a dying age now," James said.

"Should be a lot of complaints from men?" Philip asked.

"No, no trouble for our union, because you know, new cloned ladies come group by group, so males here are never angry again. I got an idea to sort out, but I'm waiting for your decision."

"Okay, I'll come to the moon in a few earth days to solve the problem of corpses. We know, there are no bacteria on the moon, so creatures can't be corrupted, but it also has no oxygen for burning. So we'll find a way, we can't pollute the moon. See you on the moon!"

Christmas was coming. Apollo Hotel did a new decoration. Alisa and Bengali stood in front of their door and sent red envelopes, food and clothes to the poor people who are standing around the door. An old man trembled and said, "You are a good person, all Apollo's people are good people!"

Alisa whispered to Bengali, "I just miss my Sma and Lis." Her eyes are wet again.

"Don't think sad things, please. Believe God, and God will bless us. Dr Philip said, Sma will be sent back, besides this, we may have our own children soon." Alisa gave Bengali a blow on the arm.

"Then come on!" with that, she left shyly.

Sma sat at the table and browsed some websites from the computer, then thought about something and suddenly remembered something so she opened the drawer, and saw a small black phone. She gladly picked up and turned on the button, but she found something was wrong and said to herself, "Where is my phone? Why it is his?"

She put the phone back in that drawer.

Philip came back. When he entered the room, Sma asked him, "It seemed a problem happened in my brain, I can't comb out the whole mess. I remembered myself working in the United Nations Scientific Ethic Committee, and my dorm is over there, why am I living here now? I remembered we took your helicopter to a small town, Marana Island, remembered the big birthday party on your Matera Island and, remember the big incident in the sea, then to Emma's Apollo Grant Hotel. Why did I become Alisa's daughter and had a twin sister? She died in an accident. I was born in Carlisle, England, and graduated from Cambridge, why did I become a middle school student in Marana town? Is that what some philosophers said 'life is just being our own vision'. Or you and I have been passed through different lives?"

Philip listened patiently to learn the mystery in her heart. Then said, "Julia, if a person is too clever, thinking too much especially more imagination, may feel like you. Don't think more and take a rest first. This is our own house, set on the beautiful Matera island. It's a big and beautiful building, with a garden, a parking site, and a helicopter. All ours.

"The kitchen and bathroom are very spacious, you live here and enjoy a quiet environment, I come to see you every day and help you cook. When you feel bored, you can call me at any time."

He went to the table, opened the drawer, took out the black mobile phone that Sma had just touched, and said, "This phone is for you to use, the battery recharges only once a year."

"Thank you, Philip. I remember I have my own phone and even remember some numbers," said Sma.

"Our phones can only go straight to each other and don't work with the social network. This is the safest undisturbed system," Philip said.

Sma felt happier after talking with Philip, she walked closer and hugged Philip for a while. Philip kissed her reluctantly, and then said "good night" and then he left.

Julia and Philip came out of their laboratory in Dan Pasha Villa. Julia said, "According to the computer drill, severe flooding will come right now."

"The global sea level has risen 0.7 meters, my Matera dorm and our Marina villa are fine, as the altitude is higher there. But Adeline's Marina is just like a bowl that surrounded by a sea dam, it's can be very dangerous," Philip said.

"Do you remember when I asked you if I came back from the moon to pick you up, which island should I be the first arriving to? Your answer was Adeline's hotel to save them first. I felt a little ominous, shouldn't have asked that stupid question," Philip continued.

"Fortunately, Adeline's Hotel is a three-story building, and there is a small hill behind the roof balcony. The problem is there is a big gap between them," he continued.

"Your casual question makes me worried about that isle town like it's really immersed in the sea. You know, I am a superstition man," Philip said.

"Nonsense! Can the sea level reach the third floor? The earth goes back to Noah's Ark era. My dear stupid man!"

"I know, I mean that tsunami break the sea bank in Marana. That's why I always say our wedding ceremony is on the moon," Philip added.

"The earth is so dangerous but humans know it too late!" Julia said sadly.

They walked randomly on the grand building, passing by the lounge room, yoga room, indoor swimming pool and series of function rooms. When they reached the inflexion point, Robots said "good night" to them and left then.

It was a beautiful bedroom, with large windows, light blue-bottomed with yellow flower curtains, rosewood table and chairs, and a pillow as long as the width of the bed and covered with a silk pillowcase. Philip had Julia's agreement and then went to the shower. Julia looked at the murals in the room with interest, there were all kinds of hangings. Suddenly, she heard a phone ring. She turned her head and looked around. Found it was not hers, so she ignored it.

But the phone keeps ringing for a long time, so she had to go to the desk, but there was no phone on it, and the sound came from the drawer. She pulled the drawer and see two mobile phones inside, one was small, black and the other big green. The black one was still flashing means it was being called. But she still ignored it. Philip came back, he knew that Julia would not touch his mobile, but still glanced cautiously at Julie, as she unwittingly looked back at him.

When Julia went to the bath, Philip quickly texted Sma. "I have some business to deal with. When it's done, I'll see you ASAP, Good night."

Julia came back, Philip helped her dry her hair and affectionately said, "Watching this beautiful hair, one hundred years is not enough."

"We've just started, why life is so short?" Julia asked.

"Heh, Julia's literature is always better than mine. Yes, our good days will be very long. By the way, I'll go to the moon the day after tomorrow; I won't be able to come back in a month."

"In fact, I just stay on the moon for only one day, which is roughly equal to one month on earth. You can come here for the weekend by yourself or with your friends. When I'm not at home, our robot driver is on standby. You can call them whatever and whenever. You can ask our robot to help you do everything," Philip added.

"Do everything? No, no matter how many robots no one can catch up to my Philip," Julia said while taking up her clothes, and she spoke again, "you take rest first, I want to do sauna again, it's funny, in the tropical area it is easier catch a cold."

"Go ahead, let the robot give you a good massage, and then I can kiss you more after your sauna." He yawned and starts snoring while speaking.

Sma hugged Philip tightly. "Where have you been last weekend? You left me here alone. You just got back today but are going to the Moon again. Your company is so busy and has no work breaks?"

Philip looked closely at Sma, as beautiful as Julia, but she had little more wrinkles on her forehead than Julia. "Do you remember when we were together last time?" asked Philip.

Sma gently flicked Philip on the shoulder and said, "That was my first time! You bad guy! That was in Apollo Grant Hotel, Adeline's house!"

"Dear Sma, you really have a good memory. When I came back from the moon, we'll go to the Apollo Hotel again."

"We should see Emma and Adeline, I miss them so much. And you said I had a good memory? There is a big problem now. It's not clear whether I'm Julia or Sma, but I can control myself and let time help me straighten out."

"Don't worry about it. This happens to people who are extremely clever. When I came back, I'll help you sort it out confidently. I'll have a long holiday and I'll take you to America to visit Emma and Adeline as well."

"I'm looking forward to it, Philip." Sma gave a warm kiss on Philip's face for a long time, but Philip was obviously less involved, just thought, *Her memory is gradually developing. last time she remembered things that happened when she was a university student and she didn't allow me to come close to her, but now, she can remember 'she' gave me her first night, but she was lacking memory between collecting her cells until becoming a kid.*

"Good morning!" Alisa greeted the guests and the waitresses.

As soon as the guests sat down at the table, they started talking about the weather, the climate.

"It's too warm this winter. One of my brothers came from Los Angeles and said the outdoor temperature was over 32 'C.'"

"We've got a risk here now, the sea level raised suddenly, a beach reef used to be one meter above sea level but was immersed into the water recently."

"Really? We're going to retreat again?"

"There are fewer and fewer places to withdraw now."

The waitress brought them tea and breakfast, two customer ladies asked Alisa about Sma and Lis, Alisa smiled bitterly and replied, "Thank you for caring, she will come back soon."

Julia sat on the desk opposite her investigators Beta and Anna. Julia asked them questions while she held a photo in her hand. "The twins' IQ is extremely uneven?" Julia asked.

"Yes, the dead one was a normal IQ. And that missing girl's IQ is too higher than normal," Beta replied.

"She got an astonishing memory ability. She can speak out that something happened before she was born, she got university acknowledgement when she just into a second school," Anna added.

"The twin IQ inequality is possible, but what you're talking about is a little weird," Julia said.

"The girl's account of her experience is unthinkable, and the names of the place she mentioned are specific and true," Anna added.

"For example, the dead girl only remembered after she was born and lived with Alisa and Bengali, but the missing girl said she was growing up in Carlisle, England."

"Carlisle!" Julia almost called out. And looked at the two girls' photo, they were exactly like herself. She was stunned. Came back to normal and then, said, "When I was in college, I once drove my teacher and two other classmates on a field trip, they talked and laughed behind me.

"I listened to them but forgot to remember road marks. When drove back at a cross, I didn't know which way to go. None of us knew that the teacher said 'Take a rest, eat and play, it may be the best way'. So I leaned my car to the side of the road, all of us got off, sat on the grass for a picnic, and watched our car from time to time. Suddenly, I saw a milk van, I met before, and remembered its dirty fender, now it was empty to go back, that was indicating we were on the correct direction so we got home very soon."

Julia carried on, "If any or both of you would like to fly with me to our Dan Pasha villa tonight for the weekend and relax there, perhaps it's easier for us to sort out this complicated mystery."

"I had a plan for the weekend, I'm sorry," said Anna.

"That would be great! I'll go with you. Should I bring some delicious food?" asked Beta.

"No, the villa has everything. Oh, let me tell the robots to get ready and fly here to pick us up."

Julia pressed her phone and got a reply immediately, a robot said, "Thank you for your command. We'll fly over at once and get to your address in 30 minutes. We will also make other preparations to make sure you'll have a happy weekend."

The helicopter landed at the Dan Pasha villa. Beta and Julia got off while the robot pilot said, "Have a nice weekend."

First, Beta glanced around, "It's a great palace! Beautiful, Brilliant! Oh, Julia, I'm sorry, I must go to the loo…"

Julia pointed to a robot on the roadside, "You can call them any time for any help!" Beta was taken to the toilet by a female-like robot.

Later, the two friends took a rest on the seats under palm trees and tasted the tea robots serviced. Beta asked, "I feel strange why there are a lot of toilets in your villa?"

Julie replied, "Yes, there are a lot of toilets. I've not yet taken the account seriously. The main purpose was to save time. Fitness toilet near the fitness room, reading toilet near the reading room and so on. And also helicopter and car parking toilet, sea shore dressing room toilet…"

"You're blessed! Philip is great!" Beta said enviously. Then the two women went to the beach dressing room and changed clothes in bikinis. Robots sent them to the water by rickshaw, as Julia had last time, there were robots in the water and drone surveillance in the air to protect them in safe hands. The two women swam in a variety of styles accompanied by robots, Julia also tried some surfing, and Beta diving to 20 meters away.

After disembarking, the two women went to the seashore dressing room and changed into dry dresses. Came out of the dressing room and went to the main building, they passed a tennis court, and Beta pulled Julia to play tennis for a while until they were tired enough like deflated balls.

Two robots came and help them and let them take a seat in the nearest dining hall. A robot said to them, "Have cool drinks to get back to life right away." Then delivered them watermelon and pineapple juice, and the two women quickly regained their spirits after drinking.

"It's immortal life here! Philip is the best man in the world!" Beta sighed.

Julia said comfortably, "If you see his appearance, just the kind of a man, nothing special."

It was a beautiful dining hall which linked to a bright clean kitchen with a transparent glass door between. Robot chef working in the kitchen and robots service in the dining hall. There were mahogany tables and chairs in the hall.

Dinner began, and a robot waiter pushed a food trolley and sent them Chicken curry, halogen pig trotters, steamed carps, Australian abalone, bananas, pineapples, champagne, and black grape drinks. Both of them touched the robot's hip and laughed very happily.

After dinner, the two walked into the garden, there were countless tropical flowers, and luxuriant branches illuminated by garden lanterns. With Beta's consent, Julia asked robot pilots to drive them to see Dan Pasha's main islands, Bali Island and Jakarta.

Through helicopter windows, they saw the white beaches below, the dark blue sea, giant ships and tiny white sails. Red walls. Green tiles everywhere, hundreds of islands and cities, in Jakarta, Bundara HI centre surrounded by beautiful buildings, roads lamps made the city like a fire dragon.

"It's so beautiful. How nice it would be, Julia, to spend every day like today!" Beta said.

"Unfortunately, our earth is in danger," said Julia sadly.

The robots carried them and navigated for a long time until the moon moved from east to west, all towns and ships already lit off, and the cool breeze invented, then they flew back to the villa.

Lying across the king-size bed, they were so tired, spread out of hands, shoes were not taken off. In only a few minutes, they went to sleep with all their clothes and without taking a shower.

There was a faint 'beep-beep' sound in the room like a bug bumping into something hard. Beta woke up first and heard it. She didn't disturb Julia but got up quietly and look around. She couldn't find out where the sound came from. She was a little nervous, just as Julia woke up.

"What time is it now? Beta, we haven't taken a shower, have we?"

"It's true, we haven't. But please listen carefully, there is a sound in this room," whispered Beta.

Julia calmed down and heard the faint sound. They looked around, and checked the floor, walls, desks and the bed, no way! Sometimes the sound would stop for a few seconds, which made them more confused. Only one thing was sure the sound absolutely happened in this room! But really don't know where it was. Both of them felt a little creeped out. Suddenly, Julia remembered what Philip said, "Robots can do anything for you". So she phoned and asked the robots for help. A robot came in, he turned his head in all directions, and soon, he ran straight to a window desk, opened a drawer and took out a small black mobile phone, and said, "Oh, that's the sound maker. This is a dedicated phone of Dr Philip's. He had forgotten to take it away. The sound is a signal that tells its battery ran out. Should I take it away and replace a new battery?" No one answered his question, so the robot took the phone away himself.

"So, it's like this!" the two ladies looked at each other and went back to bed again.

But Julia got up again and said, "You go to sleep, I'll take a shower."

"So do I!" said Beta.

"Why don't we go to the sauna together?" asked Julia.

"Yes, fine!" Beta answered briskly.

In the sauna cabin, the two ladies lay naked in a steam room for a while and then put on towels and went to the massage room, and lay on a massage bed face down, pink towels covered their back, and two male-like robots gave them a full body massage.

While the two ladies were in the sauna, the robot returned the mobile phone to their window desk. And the robot left a note by the side of the phone: "Ladies, the phone battery has been replaced, please check it. If you have any questions, please just ring me." Only later, two ladies came back and got it.

"Let me check it, the guy forgot to bring it. Perhaps the moon doesn't need it," Julia made a face as she said.

As soon as she switched it on and did not press any key, a female voice goes out, "Aren't you on the moon? Why are you calling me now?"

Julia and Beta were startled. "Who are you? Where are you?" asked Julia.

"How could it be a woman? You're not Philip? You said this is our special hotline. Why someone else today? And a woman?"

"Oh, my God!" Julia almost collapsed. Beta comforted her and told her not to rush. Julia came back in a second and said, "Philip is not like that."

"You had to ask her name," Beta suggested.

Julia then asked the woman on the phone, "What's your name, where are you?"

"My name is Julia. or Sma. I'm in the garden dormitory of Dr Philip, on Matera Island. What's your name? Where are you?" Julia didn't know what to say.

Beta took the phone from her and said, "My name is Beta, we spent a weekend in Dan Pasha Island, Indonesia."

"Oh, no wonder you woke me up in the middle night. You got the wrong number. You are in Asia, the Pacific. I am in Southern Europe, the Atlantic. We have seven hours of time gaps," replied Sma.

"Excuse me, what's the relationship between you and Mr Philip?" Beta asked.

"Normally, no stranger asks for personal information. But I'm glad to reply to this question. I'm a girlfriend of Philip and we're getting to marriage soon," Sma answered.

Julia snatched the phone back from Beta. She really wanted to scold her, but she held back and calmly said to Sma, "We're tired now. I guess you are tired too. Let's go to bed and have a talk next time?"

"Well, good night!" Sma replied.

Julia and Beta face to face, felt quite strange.

"Take rest, Beta. We must have a good rest tonight. This phone seems to give us some unexpected clues. We need to be healthy and awake to figure out the problem. We'll talk about plans tomorrow."

"Yes, Julia, take a rest!" The lights dimmed down.

On the Moon Uranium mine in the daytime. The sunshine was very strong, the sun side looked extremely white like a snow land, but the back side was totally dark.

Many cranes were working in the sunshine, lifting the soil from the uranium deposits to the surface of the ground, and workers wear spacesuits, they were using a variety of equipment to detect and analyse the composition of those soils. After their discussion, the soil was sent to different ways according to their instructions.

Most of them were poured into the green coach, which was on the track. Whenever a motorcade was fully filled with the soil, it will be driven away by the robot drivers, and the next motorcade came automatically. There was no sound, no dust. Some of the soil that did not be reaching the standard, was dumped into the red bucket car, and carried away by robots to another direction.

A convertible came; two men slowly got out of the car, they were Philip and James. They went to the crane. Looking down, there was a deep gully below, which could be imagined as a result of blasting for getting uranium soil.

"Your suggestion is correct, to bury all the dead clone ladies in abandoned mines. Then filling the gullies. There are no bacteria, corpses can't decay; no oxygen, corpses can't be burnt; burying is the only way," Philip said.

"That's a good idea. Now, can we start burying the first batch?" asked James. Philip nodded.

The robot transported clone bodies, train after train, from a distance. When Philip walked close to them, he saw the cloned female body exposed, on that top, was cloned Julia, her hair was white, and the mole on her left chin was still clear.

Philip felt a little sad, and said, "Let's give them a space prayer, although we didn't treat them as human beings. They comforted the single men on the moon and helped the human space career." The two men drew a cross on their chests and read eulogies in their mouths.

The crane gently lifted the female corpse coach and dumped them into a deep gully. Philip gently closed his eyes and shed a tear.

"How much did the second batch of clones distribute to you?" asked Philip.

"It's funny, another 6,000. It looks like a rule."

"Has any accident like 'cousin' again?"

"No, the quality was better than the first group, and employees say that cloned women had a slightly physiological response that made them more happier." James smiled.

"That's why you got a big increase in output and won a big prize!" Philip said.

"Thank you, Dr Philip, for the specifically coming."

"Oh, not at all, cloned women can only live on the moon for about 50 days, so we have to keep sending new clones, but your nourishment system needs to update and I'll help to do it."

"Well, then go and get busy." James shook hands with Philip and left. Philip called a convertible go to another way.

By the seaside avenue, Julia and Beta talked as they walked. Julia start the topic, "It's strange and complicated, the most bizarre that I am involved in it, Philip is also in it, no, my initial feeling is that Philip was the protagonist."

Beta said, "Will it be a fraud?"

"No. She's never looked for us. We first turned on the phone before her speaking. Robot and she both mentioned that's Philip's dedicated phone." Julia was sure.

"Will it be an alien? Or what kind of robot that Philip used?" Beta said oddly.

The two ladies sat down in a chair, and two female robots sent them tea and pastries. Julia looked at the robot on the left and another robot on the right. Her eyes suddenly brightened and said, "Yes! I've got an idea. We'll fly back this evening to restart working tomorrow, and then I'll visit that 'Julia'."

"Very good plan. When you need help, we'll be there in time," Beta said.

"I think, you stay in the office for dealing with the schedules, I'll tell you something in time, then use your smart brain to help me analyse the situation and gave me some advice."

"All right!"

The night on the moon was very cold. Outside the house, minus 200 centigrade. Temperature reporting screens were everywhere.

But the citizen's home was very warm and comfortable. Philip wore a sleeveless shirt, and sat in a rocking chair, having a video call with Boris. Boris' face and voice were grave. "These days, the sea level has risen another 0.4 meters. My Bali villa is level with the sea. Your Dan Pasha villa is half a meter higher than ours. But it's hard to say how long the sea rising will keep going."

"The moon really doesn't have such concerns, and the problems here are all solved, and the second batch of clones is welcomed. It will be fine to send 40,000 a year in the future. I know the pressure on the boss is very heavy to send a huge amount into the space. Only if I can succeed in my research of re-clone and clone back, we won't need to collect cells from Earth and don't need to send clones to outer space then."

"Dr Philip, if you got success in re-clone and clone back, you'll be a hero of mankind! I can't imagine what would happen in human history!"

"Yes. Each time when I think of the suppression from earth communities when I daren't tell the truth to my loved one. I was worried. Much pressure made me forget to bring my dedicated mobile with me this time. Hope it doesn't cause trouble."

"Nothing surprising! You may make mistakes when doing things! But I admire you are very sober, very calm, purposeful, and modest at any time. Please take care of yourself, don't be too tired," said Boris affectingly.

"Thank you, boss!" replied Philip.

After Boris disappeared, Philip connected Garry, "Hey, I forgot my dedicated phone at the earth home, please forward Sma's tracking video for me."

"Okay, it's coming."

Philip opened the video, surprised to see Julia and Sma, greeting each other sitting together in Matera Island's garden dorm.

Sma, with slight wrinkles on her forehead, face to face with her original person, Julia. Julia looked friendly, listened to her, and occasionally interrupted a little. When Sma paused for a while, Julia said, "It looks like that our story begins in the town of Marina, and we have to go there together."

"Well, Julia, I'll do what you think," Sma said.

After seeing this video, Philip called Garry, "Please continue to watch it. Without that specific phone, I can't see Sma directly and can't contact her, and can't contact my Julia. But I'm going back to Earth right now."

Garry answered, "Okay, I'll do what you said."

It was sunset, but the sunshine still could be seen from building gaps. So early the neon light of the Apollo Grant Hotel was been shining. Through the windows, it could be seen how busy the business they do. Waitresses were busy in the restaurant hall. All tables were fully occupied. Customers come out or come in constantly. Alisa greeted them with a smile, most of them were acquaintances.

Bengali in a beautiful waistcoat, a yellow tie, and a standard hairstyle, constantly appeared in the hall and greeted everyone.

At one table, three men drank and talked about tuna on the plate. "I heard that tuna is getting cheaper and cheaper now, they say that the temperature underwater is too high, marine animals were seriously hurt and even can't swim so it's easier to be caught," one man said.

"Did you hear a news reported by TV yesterday? A big group of dolphins migrant to our sea shore, Scientists do not yet know why."

"Don't just think about animals, think about our human selves now! Maybe we are the last residents on the earth. We don't know tomorrow, just for today, though."

"Huge years later, who could know that we used to live and work hard on earth? Imagine those stars in the sky, perhaps they had stories and were just like us. Earth's fools trusted scientists, but now, scientists can do nothing."

Alisa warmly welcomed two new ladies, she was astonished when she recognised one of them is Sma, "Isn't that Sma?"

Sma, too, affectionately rushed over and cried, "Mom, it's been so long." And shed tears. Alisa burst into tears with joy, and the two hugged each other. Julia stood by and was surprised.

Alisa turned around and looked at Julia, and said, "You, you? You shouldn't be Lis?"

Bengali came towards here and suddenly stopped and then hesitantly went back and came again, he said to Alisa, "You take ladies upstairs, arrange for them to eat and rest, chat with them. I'll be in charge of the hall instead of you tonight."

Sma and Julia followed Alisa to go upstairs and into a mini cabin restaurant where Sma used to have dinner with Lis. Alisa said, "You two sit down, I'll go to bring some drinks."

"You see, Julia, when I am here, I became Sma, the daughter of Bengali and Alisa, here I had primary and middle school, and had a twin Lis, Lis was crushed to death. I was locked up in a little, dark room before I was taken away by Philip. He picked me up on the same day after Lis was dead," speaking of this, Sma could not help but burst into tears.

She continued, "But another life in my memory was born in the United Kingdom, home town, Carlisle. Graduated from Cambridge and had a job in the UN Science Ethics Committee."

She told Julia a lot of things happened here.

Alisa brought them volcano-brand drink, lobster, rabbit meat, and pizza, and said to Sma, "They are all your favourite."

Sma hurried to grab it with her hand and gobbled, Julia used a knife and fork and ate decently.

Alisa wanted to find a chance to have a talk with Sma alone, but there was no chance. So she had to say, "It's good you are back, we missed you too much. Would you like to live in a double room with her or two single rooms?"

Sma, look at Julia, Julia said, "It's up to you."

So Sma said, "Let's live in my room. Okay?"

Alisa said, "Of course, my princess Sma." saying this, she went away.

Sma invited Julia to go to her bedroom after dinner. They walked into a beautiful room; the environment was relaxing and pleasant. There were blue orchids that Sma and Julia both liked on the dressing table. Julia was very happy but Sma said, "No, which room is mine? It's a little messy. I remember having a small room next to Lis, and another bigger room with Dr Philip for one night. And all in this hotel."

In the chance, Alisa was not here, Sma stretched out her head and looked out of the corridor, pointed to a room in the distance and whispered to Julia, "That's the room, where I gave my virgin to Philip."

Julia's face flushed when she heard this. But regained her composure quickly and said to Sma, "It's still early, why don't we go for a walk on the roof balcony?"

"A balcony? I've heard of it, but I hadn't gone there. My parents are afraid to allow us to go there. Oh, by the way, that small room they locked me in should be near the balcony. Let's go. I'll show you."

As she climbed to the third floor, Sma looked left and right to find that small room where she was locked.

When Julia heard such things, she had some questions in mind and sent a message to Beta saying, "She remembered all my experiences, but was lacking memory about the balcony. Obviously, she doesn't know what happened after that day, indicating that Philip collected my somatic cells on that day. But she knew something which I don't know that she experienced herself since being sent to Marana town until today."

Beta then wrote back: "Note how she interacts with Philip after that night. Find out when she started to be Alisa's daughter."

"Hey, Julia, I found a secret room," Sma called Julia in a low voice.

Julia followed her passed two corners and into a dark windowless room with only a small bed, a small table and a short candle lying on the table. "When you were locked here? How long?"

"I was locked on that day Lis was crushed, and I was released until Philip took me away. Oh, that was on the same day after Lis died and Mom was rescued by an ambulance. And, sorry, I forgot it, it was a helicopter. I didn't want to go, at last, my dad and mum carried me into the helicopter, but don't remember where the helicopter was parked."

"How about that room where you slept with Philip, can you remember clearly?"

"It should be clear. Let's go over and have a look."

They walked down into that room Julia was familiar with an unforgettable place.

"You two got up quite late that day, right?" Julia asked Sma.

"I can't remember that," speaking of that, Sma felt a little dizzy.

"Sit down and take a break." Julia made her a cup of juice from the table. "Remember what you did after you got up?" Looking at the recovery of Sma's face, Julia asked, Sma shook her head.

Julia just want to ask more, Alisa gently came in, "Tell you a big news, Emma and Adeline, our boss just arrived at the hotel, do you want to see her?"

"That's great!" the two women answered simultaneously, seeing this, Alisa was puzzled.

Emma and Adeline seemed a little tired and sat where they had last time. Alisa served them a hot drink and just want to speak something, Julia and Sma come in, and all people in the room were surprised and excited.

But then Emma and Adeline were confused, as didn't know what to do. The two 'Julia' called their names, "Emma,

Adeline" at the same time. Both hugged them. Alisa was very happy to see this, but then shook her head and left bewildered.

"Julia, you have twins?" Adeline asked, actually she didn't know who was Julia though. The two looked at each other. Julia just gave out an "n" voice, but Sma said, "Yes, but my twin, Lis, was crushed by a car." Her words made Emma and Adeline more confused.

Adeline and Emma pointed to Julia and asked Sma, "Who is she?"

Just at this moment, Bengali came in, and made a respectful call to Adeline, "Boss, my dear wife!"

Adeline, eager to get an answer about Julia, turned to Bengali, "Could you help to figure it out?"

"Sure, I'll tell you clearly and tell the whole family to understand," Bengali said.

"You, Bengali, have really changed! You can hold a lot of things in your stomach now! Hi, Bengali, it's time to close shop now? Let the whole staffs come and reunited together!"

"Okay!" Bengali readily replied.

Together with Alisa, three waitresses quickly made a big table with a new tablecloth, placed plenty of drinks, fruits, dishes, tuna, lobster and pizza. People sat around, enjoy delicious dinner and talked with each other. Adeline raised her glass, "Thanks to Julia and Dr Philip, our forever friends, and to Alisa and all staff, your excellent working made the hotel back to glory!" Everybody raised their glass.

"I am accompanying Emma to the Rome International Hotel Research Institute today. I grabbed a chance to come here to see you all. Can you tell us the secrets now, Bengali? It's family here."

Bengali looked around with a little hesitation.

"Boss lady asked you, so you should say it out," Alisa encouraged him. Julia wanted to listen to it very much, their faces flushed and their eyes fixed on Bengali.

"All right! If I don't clarify it, a lot of things may confuse all family here. Do you remember the day we went to the old boss's grave? The clone company and the cloned old boss?" Adeline and all staff nodded, Sma looked at a loss, and Julia realised this.

Bengali went on in his speech, "Alisa and I always be grateful to Dr Philip, who helped Alisa from birth defects with cloning technology. And he also asked me to do him a favour that was to keep a pair of girls here."

Julia suddenly remembered that picture of the twin girls.

"What happened later?" Sma asked because she remember that photo was taken of her and Mom and Lis.

"They looked like twins, both of them got a mole on their left chin. But Dr Philip told me it was his experimental study, he said. The girls will be growing 25 times quicker than normal people, the two children may be different in intelligence, and that he has skills to monitor them any time."

"What happened later?" Emma asked in great surprise.

"Sma was very talented, swiftly moving to secondary from primary school, and she even knew more knowledge than college students, and she said, her hometown in Carlisle, Britain!"

Sma stood up in shock. "So that! It was me! Then what?"

Sma shed tears, and her forehead was sweating, Julia helped her to calm down.

"Later, Dr Philip suddenly called me to lock Sma, and said he'll come to pick her up, he would also pick up Lis, too, but Lis died in a car accident when she ran away with Alisa."

Hearing this, neither Alisa nor Sma couldn't control their tears. Emma and Julia wept and help wipe the tears of Alisa and Sma. Other female employees all shed tears.

"So far, but you've missed the point. Dr Philip asked you to help, and he must have told you the biggest secret?" said Adeline, and the muttered employees immediately in quiet, waiting for Bengali to speak.

Bengali stopped for a while, drew a cross on his chest and spoke slowly, "He only told me that the two girls were clones."

"Well, that's impossible!" Julia and Sma both stood up. But Julia thought of something, flushed and sat down slowly, while Sma burst into tears.

"I'm sorry, everyone, I know now, I'm not a human being, but I am a human being. I'm a cloned human being."

She looked at Julia with tears, Julia hugged her suddenly. Sma suddenly collapsed and everyone panicked.

Someone suggested calling for an ambulance. Bengali said, "No, she's in a special situation. Don't get into trouble. Please keep the secret today. I can't help to tell you the truth and hope it is not a betrayal to Dr Philip. We are always grateful to him."

Adeline said, "It's not your fault, it's a good thing to make clear. It's all God's plan. Since it shows up, Sma is one of us. As the same as Julia, Emma and Alisa, deserve respect and love."

"Boss lady is right!" everyone agreed.

"Julia, Bengali and Alisa, you can keep talking. Emma and I should catch the flight. Sma will be fine. For a moment of mental stimulation, anyone will be the same. Well, God will arrange everything." Emma ran to Julia, hugged her for a while, and hugged Sma, then made a farewell to everyone.

Later, Sma woke up but still sat on the ground. Bengali and Alisa fed her tea, gently called her name, and whispered to her. Taking this opportunity, Julia ran out of the hall and sent information to Beta and said, "It's obvious that her memory of my character ended early that day after sleeping with Philip, and then her memory was blank until she was a student in Marana schools. She doesn't know graveyard things. And the time she started school was when I got that twins' photo."

"Finally, Bengali locked Sma and Lis crushed on the same day when you were investigating them. It is clear that Philip collected my cells on that day we slept in the Marina Hotel, and he used my cells to create clones. You come right now. We'll ask the sheep cloning guys for help. Please ask them to bring related equipment for identifying use," Julia gave Beta a task.

Beta, Julia and Sma were waiting in a reception room at the sheep clone company.

It was a strong wind and torrential rain outside. Thunder, lightning, one after one. Suddenly a very horrible thunder made the three women almost jump up.

"A thunderstorm in south Europe is so heavy that I've never known," Beta said.

"There was almost never such thunder in our hometown of Carlisle, even though there was drizzling a lot," Sma said, and Julia nodded. Beta glanced at Julia.

Suddenly, the lights went out and the room became dark. "It's so scary!" Beta said. Julia pulled out her phone, its screen brightened the room, so they could see each other then. Sma suggested Julia to turn it off, "It's dangerous to turn it in lightning!"

At this time, a small rear door opened, and someone said, "I'm sorry, the electrician will quickly fix the problem and light you candles first now. The clone expert you want to meet with was stuck on the road by the heavy rain, but he will be here soon."

The candlelight made everyone smile. "Think of the ancient times, the era of natural life. Drilling for fire, wax lighting is a luxury!" sighed Beta.

"But if science and technology hadn't been developed, how can clones be born?" Sma said, it amused Julia and Beta, and Sma herself, she couldn't help laughing.

The sounds of rain decreased and the electric lights come again. Everyone felt better.

Outside came the sound of a car parking, and then the front door was pushed open and walked in two men, they were acquaintances for both Julia and Beta, and they were from Sheep Clone Company. Julia, Beta and Sma stood up and shook hands with them. The fat and short man said, "Please come in and have a seat."

The three ladies followed them and went through a small door into a reception room with sofas, coffee tables, and bonsai. Inexplicable paintings of ancient myths or science fantasies on the walls. Two ladies came over from the reception desk and handed over drinks to everyone.

The fat and short man said to Julia, "We haven't met for a long time. How is everyone?"

Beta specifically introduced Julia's position. "She, Julia, is the head of the United Nations Commission on Ethics in Science and Technology."

"Welcome, Ms Julia, we've met," the two men said at the same time, Sma turned her head and looked at Julia.

"Is that lady a twin of Ms Julia?" said the short fat man.

The tall man shook his head and said, "No, according to my professional perception, if there are no chronic diseases, such as digestive or endocrine disease, she is very likely to be Ms Julia's clone."

"What?" His speech was like a bomb shot all people here…

"Chock! Don't be too bookish, don't forget Ms Julia's identity," said the short fat man quietly, but the house echoed his voice loud enough that everyone heard it.

"Oh, don't think about that, we have no other purpose. Mr Chock, you are very professional, we may have to admit, you are correct! She is my clone. Can you tell us firstly why you felt that way?" Julia asked him calmly.

"What I have said is not really believable. According to my observation, the colour wavelength of the clones is different to the original people, for example, white, the white of the clone is like a dried bone, but the original person's white is like a white feather of a live bird."

All the audience here including Julia and Sma, compared their own complexion, Sma seemed a bit unstable.

"Mr Chock, last time we saw cloned Adeline's father, it was nothing like a real person, but my clone has everything like me, soul, language and memory. Where's your clone?" asked Julia.

"That clone's resistance is very weak, like a thin tissue, very easy to be broken. After we met at the cemetery, he died in the covid-19 pandemic," All people here felt pity.

"Can you tell us in common language, Mr Chock, the basic process of human cloning?" Beta asked.

"Well, collect the cells from a normal person, check the cells whether useful or not, or aught it, or put male's mixed females and then nourish the cells for growing until become fatal," Chock replied.

"So why someone didn't know body cells were collected but it really happened?" Beta continued asking.

Chock thought a little bit, then replied, "That perhaps moral ethics involved like a thief. For example, collect cells while that original person into sleep or any reason made him unconscious."

Julia and Beta exchanged glances to show what they understood. Then Beta asked Chock, "Mr Chock, can you explain why Adeline's father's clone was like a doll, but Julia's clone is like Julia herself as you see here?"

"I am very ashamed as I'm not reached such a high level. Maybe we only collected cells from the newly dead, and her clone was collected from a living human. But it may not be so simple. I can't guess the secret of others. So we can only do sheep cloning business at the moment," Chock said.

"The cloning of Adeline's father was just a whim, and we have given up. I heard someone has cloned humans with thought, language, and consciousness. Unexpectedly, she is in front of me today!" Chock said in admiration.

Sma listened in tears, wanting to open her mouth but stopped as Julia asked Chock a new question. "Have you ever heard of Matera's Boris?" said Julia.

"Oh, Matera Boris! It's the world's most well-known organ-cloning company; they can clone human skin, teeth, hair and internal organs. Yes, someone saying that they can clone out real people," said Chock.

"Mr Chock, can I ask you another question? You're referring to the feather, the dried bone, what's the main reason?" said Julia.

"Ms Julia, for the subject, all from my intuitive feeling but can't make sense. It may be linked to cell divisions, for example, a normal person's cell can be divided 25 times, but clones depend on technicians, perhaps quite a few times and, such cells were forced to grow very fast despite lacking full nutrition. So their colour wavelength and their life is…" He was scrupled about the existence of Sma. And stopped halfway.

"Mr Chock, I am confident that I am part of Julia's body. I believe in scientific truth and am not afraid of accidents. The main purpose of today is to ask you to help us test whether Julia and I have a relationship of cloning. Please help with this big favour." Sma took the initiative to break Chock's concerns.

Chock asked his assistant to put the toolbox on a table. He pulled out a chair from under the table and sat down.

Open the toolbox, and took out two small rectangle boxes, he goes to Julia, asked her to open her mouth, and he took out a small cotton stick from the small box, rolled her tongue, then immediately insert the stick into a tiny glass tube, and covered that box. Then did the same on Sma, then he went back to his table, plugged the two pipes into different plugs and let the computer operate itself.

During the waiting time, people watch the weather outside the house, it's raining again, but the sun is shining at the same time. The help desk lady came again and sent them hot drinks.

"Now I'm declaring the test results for you: Sma is a clone of Ms Julia, and Sma is the 'ultimate cell', which means, it's not possible to continue splitting, that is, her usual life can only be one in 25th of a normal people. I'm so sorry. But that's what the data is."

Sma snuggled Julia sadly, but instead of crying, she said, "No worry, don't be sad, since you're alive, I feel happy enough." Back to Julia, she burst into tears, and the sound of sobs filled in the whole room.

Mr Chock and his assistant tied up the equipment and got up, saying, "Madam, if there's nothing else, we're going to say goodbye now. We must be moving all sheep to safe heights, this island is going to sink soon."

Beta and Julia stand up and shook hands with the two men and watch them leave.

Julia, Beta and Sma are still sitting there. Beta said, "It is clear that Dr Philip is a successful scientist who cloned human beings with souls, memories, and language totally as normal people. Which would be a great contribution to mankind. However, there are many questions that need to be discussed such as the aspect of morality and ethics. He loved his fiancée but collected his fiancée's cells without prior consent. What happens if this cloning technology were used by bad people, such as war traffickers and drug dealers?"

"Yes, you're right, and to me, he's also responsible for breaking his word because he knew I'd been against immoral science," Julia said.

Suddenly, Sma knelt on the ground and said in tears, "I beg you to forgive my loved Philip, don't punish him because he cloned me. He is the creator of my life. He let me know the ups and downs of a human's life, and let me see the colourful world. I loved him deeply." with words, she burst into tears. Beta and Julia were blurry in tears too, and Julia said in cried,

"You and I are both in love with this man, aren't I deeply in love with him?"

Beta turned her tearful face toward the window and said to Julia and Sma, "You two take a rest and stay in this town for a night, and I'll fly leaving now. We wouldn't do the discussion of a moral problem before Julia gets back, okay?"

Julia nodded and said, "Well, you go first, we'll go back tomorrow. Since Philip oversees Sma, he'll know I'm here, and he'll come to here to see us. I'll ask him to extend Sma's life, and make us real twins."

"Yes!" said Sma and Beta. The rain stopped, and sunshine come in through the window. The three ladies left their seats, say "goodbye" to reception and left.

Apollo Hotel. In a big bed. Julia and Sma cuddled each other and shared one pillow. Strong wind roaring outside and heavy rain beat windows.

Sma said, "Don't know when Philip will pick us up. It's not convenient for him as he left the phone at home."

Julia burst into tears and swallowed, "My heart is very tired now, and have a good chat tomorrow."

"Obey you, Julia. I'm a cell from you. Good night." They two kissed each other and the lights dimmed.

An explosion woke them up and they quickly sat up. They switched the lights on, but it's not working. Outside windows, no street lights could be seen. With the grey sky, they could see dark shadows of buildings, but such shadows showed that some buildings have collapsed.

Then, there were noises coming from inside the hotel, guests complained no light was on, and children and women cried. Julia and Sma immediately got up and want to open the door to see what happened. Surprised them that flooding water has been into their room and their shoes were floating away. Julia turned on her phone and could see the flood has been reached their knees. The door was not easier to open as water forced it.

"Disaster!" Julia shouted. "Come on, rescue the guests and children!" she said in a calm voice. Then the two women found their shoes, they tried hard opened the door and held hands, touched the wall out of their room.

There've been candles lit in some rooms. Some adult guests left their rooms and went out through the water. Bengali and Alisa were helping family guests, elderly people and children. They tied the children to floating wood furniture.

Bengali crashed some wooden doors to get a board for rescue guests and carefully lifted the elderly to such board and said to them, "That's all, God bless!"

Julia and Sma also helped them evacuate several guests' families. But the water level was getting higher and higher and reached the waist.

Alisa clasped Bengali without any words; Bengali said to her, "Thank God, I had a sweet time with Alisa for so many days. I can die smiling." He lifted Alisa's chin and then they kissed each other feverishly.

"Come on, Alisa, Julia and Sma, let's go to the roof. We should be saved. Everyone must be living!"

Julia and Sma followed them and walked through the water, grabbing railings and climbing step by step. At last, they arrived at the top of the building, through a doorstep, they come down to the roof balcony. stood on the balcony, overlooking the streets below, it's like a surging river: crashed furniture, dead animals, and people's bodies were floating on it and washed forward by the stream. surprised them more was, can't believable, turtles and snakes were swimming, seabirds and dolphins make out different sounds like wolves howling in grief, all such species treat the town as a sea.

"Plea Philip come quickly. Just get Julia out of here. I'm willing to die," Sma said.

"No, we are bundled life, you'll live as I live. You are the ultimate cell, need first protection, and then let Philip study re-cloning to extend your life. My cells can be divided many times, even if I died, my somatic cells can clone many Julia like you." Julia affectionately helped Sma tie her messy hair.

The water is raising swiftly that climbed equally to the balcony! This is the top of the three-floor building's roof! Except for a few high buildings, all of the streets have disappeared, and the small hill behind the balcony and the cork oak on its slope still can be seen, except for that hill, the town seemed almost connected with the sea.

Now the flooding has risen to their feet, Bengali said to Alisa, "Honey, when we struggled to float over the sea, we both won. Today we'll gamble again. Go to the rail, and pick up the wood planks or plastic panels for life-saving. When we see the floating wooden door or such things, just climb it, we live or die together."

"We also pray for Emma and Adeline to be safe!" Bengali and Alisa draw a cross on their chest. Suddenly, a big wooden post floated along the rail, Bengali and Alisa immediately dragged it and shouted to Julia and Sma to climb on.

"Thank you both. Go by yourself. We are waiting. Philip will come and pick us up." Julia said.

"Then take care of yourself. God bless you!" The couple climbed on the wood and float away by that streaming.

The water level continued to rise, reaching their knees, and later, the balcony railing was nearly immersed.

Julia once again helped Sma, clean up her clothes and said affectionately, "You are a part of my life. If there is any danger, I will protect you first."

Sma cried loudly and hugged Julia, "No, dear Julia, you are the root of my life. If any danger happens, sacrifice me and keep you that were in accordance with God's will."

Suddenly, Julia's phone rang, the caller was Garry. "Are you Julia? Philip asked me urgently to find you, I'm in Matera laboratory, where are you now?"

Julia was overjoyed and replied, "Sma and I are waiting for Philip on the roof balcony, Apollo Hotel he knows."

A few seconds later, Garry called back, "Yes, I see you two. Please don't move. Dr Philip will be arriving in about half an hour."

"We're saved!" The two ladies cried bitterly.

The flood rose much faster than expected. In a blink, the water reached their chests of them, and they could not stand firmly. Julia said, "We can't be waiting to die, find things to save ourselves. We have to be alive when Philip arrived."

They held hands together in the water, keeping standing there to avoid moving. But the flood rushed too strong that separated them. Just then, a door board floated closer to Sma, Sma rushed to grab it while calling for Julia, as soon as her hand touched the board, her feet slide and she fell down in the water…

"Sma!" With a scream, Julia immediately swam to Sma and, dived into the water to help Sma stand up, then she swam to catch that board, she herself slide down a few times and grabbed the board again and again, finally drew the board back.

As soon as she was about to stand up, she was washed down by the streaming. Sma immediately rushed to help her to get it again.

Unfortunately, the board is too narrow that only can carry one person. the two ladies push it to each other, but none of them would accept it …

So they tried to move the plank across both of their chests so that sharing its floating power, but its floating force was too weak that can't afford two ladies, after struggling for a while, Sma was getting weak, Julia realised it and helped her lie face down on the plank, and told her to keep legs paddling to help buoyancy.

"Once Philip finds your wide back, he could rescue you quickly." Said Julia, and she herself kept swimming and following the board. It's lucky, Julia seized a floating pillar, so she drew it and relying upon its buoyancy, swam side to side with Sma, in a position of parallel. While swimming, Julia looked at the sky, sometimes thinking it was Philip but was sea birds.

Sma gradually lost her strength and could not continue paddling… she said to Julia in a faint voice, "Julia, can you let me call you my sister?"

Julia was stunned, and then burst into tears and said, "OK. But it's okay. I'm here. You'll be fine."

"Good sister. I'm your cell. I love you and Philip." She was pale and powerless, couldn't talk any more.

"Sma!" Julia cried loudly, then loosened her pillar, moving after Sma, little by little she paddled to keep Sma on board safe.

Suddenly she realised it was far away, deviating from the balcony and had to swim back to let Philip be easier to find them. It's too hard to swim opposite to the streaming, but she insisted on doing it.

Philip drove his helicopter over the vast flood and find Marina's geographic address, he felt so sad as everything in the beautiful town disappeared. He found the small hills with coconut trees, cork oak trees and a lawn. He knew the balcony will be nearer. But where is it?

"Where is Julia?" His eyes blurred, his heart beating fast.

Suddenly, he found her not too far from the hill but quite deviated from the balcony place. He saw a person paddling and pushing a board desperately. Someone was lying on the board face down. He was sure that the paddle lady was Julia. He said to himself, "Must rescue her first!"

But he needed Julia to show her back. He pulled the joystick to the lowest position and let the helicopter very close to the surface of the water.

He stretched his head out of the window and shouted loudly, calling Julia's name.

Maybe Julia didn't hear it. Maybe she didn't have the strength to answer. She just pushed the wooden door feebly.

"You climb to the plank! I need you back to shoot the bullet!" She did not answer and continued to paddle, more and more slowly.

Her hands suddenly loosened from that plank. She sank and did not struggle.

Philip shouted as hard as he could, "I need you back!" Philip was sweating and coughing, and couldn't continue shouting. But Julia disappeared, and there was silence.

He continued to fly around but only could see the vast sea, occasionally drifting clothes, bodies, and furniture, but no Julia. He was full of tears, and his heart was full of Julia's appearance, her voice, her song, and all her memories.

He saw the floating door and the clone lying on it, showing her back. It was pushed by Julia in the wrong direction but quite near the small hill. He gnawed his teeth and flew away.

The boiling sea made sea birds very excited; they could easily pick food from the floating farmer animals, and human bodies and pack foods.

Sma's plank was still rippling in a corner near the small hill. Seabirds began to fly above her, detecting what she was.

After a while, Philip flew back, his face showing how unwilling he was. Just as the seabirds were ready to pick Sma, he shot a bullet into Sma's back and lifted her from danger.

Just when he rescued Sma, he heard strange sounds below, and then he saw a group of large dolphins swimming toward that small hill, and together, they pushed something – like a human body to the lawn, "Julia!"

He carefully flew above them and almost stopped his breath, it was Julia! He concentrated on catching a good chance just to find Julia back, and he shot a bullet immediately. He rescued Julia. All dolphins raised their head to the sky, crying or singing.

On the moon, near a beautiful domed palace, Philip and Julia, and Sma got off a convertible. Julia and Sma were particularly beautiful in lunar clothes.

"Dear, Philip, I know that my life is only about 40–50 days on the moon. But I got love from you and Julia; you created and rescued me, thank you forever."

She burst into tears and buried her head in Philip's arms. Philip's tears hung like beads on his cheeks, and he replied, "Dear Sma, sorry, we only can call your name like this. I'd thank you forever. I was so selfish if I didn't fly back to rescue you, I'd have lost my Julia forever..." he kissed Sma enthusiastically and then he said, "I'll follow my Julia's command, to do my best to extend your life and as long as ourselves."

"Hi, Philip, I'd give you one of my approval. Sma and me, you would have two wives, are you agree?" Philip was stunned.

"Say, yes or no?" Julia said in pursuit of him while he was running away.

The End

Milton Keynes UK
Ingram Content Group UK Ltd.
UKHW020736191123
432823UK00012BA/276